"I THINK YOU'VE HAD ABOUT ENOUGH, HARRY."

"I'm not Harry, damn it. I'm George. And who the hell are you?"

"I'm the guy who's suggesting it would be a fine idea if you was to sleep it off now. By yourself. Okay, Harry?" Longarm took a firm grip above George's elbow, and squeezed. From a distance, the contact probably looked like a friendly little gesture, but George suddenly went pale and his knees became a mite loose and rubbery.

"Hey, mister, that—"

"Tell the lady good-bye now, Harry. It's time for you and your buddy to leave."

"Damn, I . . ."

"Say it, Harry."

"Yes, sir, I . . . I'm real sorry, lady, but my friend and I will be running along now."

"Nice to have this chat, I'm sure," the woman said.

"Good-bye, Harry," Longarm said. "Don't get lost on your way back to the hotel now."

"Yeah, I, uh . . ."

"Harry."

"Yes, sir?"

"One thing. I notice you have a palm gun in your left-hand coat pocket. A .32 or something inoffensive like that? I want you to know, Harry, that if you even think about taking it out to admire it, I will put a .44 slug smack between your horns. Do you take my meaning, Harry?"

TABOR EVANS

LONGARM

AND THE CRYING CORPSE

J

JOVE BOOKS, NEW YORK

LONGARM AND THE CRYING CORPSE

A Jove Book / published by arrangement with
the author

PRINTING HISTORY
Jove edition / March 1997

The Putnam Berkley World Wide Web site address is
http://www.berkley.com/berkley

ISBN: 0-515-12031-6

A JOVE BOOK®
Jove Books are published by The Berkley Publishing Group,
200 Madison Avenue, New York, New York 10016.
JOVE and the "J" design are trademarks
belonging to Jove Publications, Inc.

PRINTED IN THE UNITED STATES OF AMERICA

10 9 8 7 6 5 4 3 2 1

LONGARM

AND THE CRYING CORPSE

Chapter 1

Longarm knew damn good and well he was dreaming. The fact that he was aware that it was a dream did nothing to take away from the pleasure. In his dream there was warmth. Yellow sunlight. Green meadows. And a redheaded woman with tits like Rocky Ford muskmelons—except softer and smoother, of course—and a snatch every bit as wet, sweet, and juicy as the pale flesh of one of those same melons—except warmer, of course—and she wanted him. In the dream he knew she wanted him. Needed him. Practically cried out for him to take her, use her, plunge hip-deep inside her. She leaned close. Opened her mouth. Said . . .

"Goddammit!"

Longarm frowned. That was not exactly what a fine redheaded lady was supposed to say. He wrinkled his nose and smacked his lips and wriggled around a bit in search of a more comfortable position on the iron-hard upholstery of the Union Pacific passenger coach. Now if only he could get back to that dream and, more to the point, to that redhead . . .

"Goddammit all to hell an' back," the voice, a de-

1

cidedly masculine voice, said for the second time.

Longarm wished whoever it was would shut the hell up. That was a mighty fine dream the son of a bitch was ruining. He tried to remind himself exactly where the dream had left off. The redheaded woman was naked, right? Or was she? Dammit, he couldn't visualize her any longer.

"I insist we go ahead," another voice said.

"Insist all you damn please. Put it in writing. You want the name and address of the president of the railroad? I'll write it down for you."

"I'll have you fired if you don't get me to Cheyenne on time," the complainer whined.

"Then I expect I'm going to be fired, mister, because there sure God ain't none of us making it into Cheyenne or any other place tonight. It'll be this time tomorrow if you're damn lucky, and that's that."

Longarm opened his eyes. He might as well. His sleep was gone and so was the redheaded woman. Just as well, though. The dream woman had been so sexy he might've come in his drawers just from thinking about her, and wouldn't that have been an embarrassment for a grown man. He hadn't done any such thing like that since he was . . . he tried to think back . . . thirteen? fourteen? Along about that ridiculously randy age, if he remembered correctly.

With a yawn and a broad stretch that chattered his jaw muscles and made his shoulders fairly ache, he sat up, blinking and trying to figure out what the problem was here.

The U.P. eastbound was stationary. That was one of the first things a fellow had to notice. The train was supposed to be clattering along the tracks somewhere between Evanston, Wyoming, which was the last station he recalled stopping at, and . . . how long had he been

2

asleep? He made a rough guess without bothering to consult the key-wind Ingersoll in his pocket, and decided they couldn't be as far as Laramie yet or he would be feeling a good bit more rested than was the case. All right, then, somewhere between Evanston and Laramie. Which gave him several hundred miles of leeway.

Wherever they were, there should be a sign on the depot platform. The coach windows were fogged over solid, so he rubbed his palm in a small circle to clear some of the frozen rime.

And found himself looking into a whipping, swirling mass of white.

Sometime since they'd pulled out of Evanston they'd gone and found one helluva snowstorm, it looked like.

Longarm yawned again and stretched some more. Up toward the front of the coach a couple of businessmen were arguing with the U.P. conductor. Toward the back, where the coal-fired stove was purring and chuckling, the rest of the passengers were concentrating on keeping warm. And for a fact, it was cold as a whore's heart inside the coach. Now that he was awake and paying attention, Longarm wished to hell he was back in that dream. If not for the redheaded woman, then for the sunshine and greenery of the place where he and that horny redhead had been romping. Damn, but it was cold now that he was paying attention to the fact.

Up toward the front of the car the conductor dropped his voice to a whisper and leaned close to the face of one of the argumentative passengers. Longarm couldn't overhear what the conductor said, but he was pretty sure the conductor was one feisty little sonuvabitch, because even though the passenger was half a head taller and likely thirty pounds the heavier, it was the passenger who went kind of pale and reeled a step backward.

3

"Do I make myself clear?" the conductor asked in a normal voice.

"I guess."

"Do I? Or do you want me to prove it?" the conductor demanded.

"You make yourself clear," the passenger conceded. "I understand."

"Thank you." The conductor gave the unhappy passenger a fake smile that wouldn't have fooled a toddler, and turned to face the rest of the car. Raising his voice so he could be heard throughout, he announced, "Everybody will be getting off here, folks. There's snow blocking the tracks in the Bird Creek Cut on up the line, and nothing will be moving until the plows can clear the blockage and the dispatchers get things sorted out again. The Union Pacific will put you all up at the Jennison Arms—that's at the road's expense, mind—for as long as it takes. The telegraph lines are still open, so if anyone needs to inform your families or employers or whoever about the layover, feel free. The Union Pacific will pay for one message for each of you, up to . . . well, I don't recall how many words you're allowed, but the telegraph operator will know. If you want to claim your luggage to use during your stay here, there will be someone in the baggage compartment to help you. And don't bother asking me when the tracks will be clear again, because I surely don't know any more about that than you do." The conductor smiled—it looked like the genuine article this time—and added, "If anybody wants to get into a betting pool on what time the wheels move east again, see me in the lobby of the Jennison Arms once we're all settled. And by the way, heavy as that snow is blowing out there, I suggest we all move from the train to the hotel in one group. I'd hate for anybody to get lost and freeze to death between the platform and the inn.''

Longarm tried to look outside again, but the spot he'd rubbed clear only a few moments earlier was already frosted over and completely opaque again. It could be that the conductor wasn't bullshitting about the danger of a person getting lost and frozen if he didn't know where he was going.

Where *was* he going? Longarm wondered where the hell he was.

For some reason the name Jennison Arms kind of struck a chord. He'd either stayed there before, taken a meal there, or at least been somehow familiar with it in the past. If he could just remember . . . hell, yes. Jennison Arms. Longarm hadn't stayed there before, but he'd eaten at the hotel restaurant.

The train was stopped in Kittstown, Wyoming, not too awful far west of Medicine Bow and about a like distance east from Rawlins. He'd been here—what? A year and a half ago? Something like that. Came up to claim a prisoner on federal warrants and got acquainted with Town Marshal Clay Waring and his wife. What the hell was her name anyhow? Marjorie, that was it. Clay and Marjorie Waring. Helluva nice couple. That was why he hadn't had to stay at the Jennison Arms. The Warings took him into their home and fed him and sat up talking half the night with him, and the next day he stood treat for them for a fancy meal at the hotel.

Oh, he remembered now, all right. It'd been their wedding anniversary and Clay had forgotten it, and Marjorie was going to cloud up and get her feelings hurt until Longarm pretended he'd talked Clay out of his own celebration plans and insisted on the best meal in town to honor the special occasion. Yeah, Longarm recalled it now. Nice visit that had been. Nice folks. And if he

5

was going to have to spend some more time in Kitts-town, well, he would just have to look up Clay and Marjorie and make a pleasure out of the layover.

"Get your things together, everyone," the conductor called from the front of the car. "Get ready to leave. I'll be back in a few minutes with the people from the other car. Please be ready when I return. We wouldn't want anyone lost, ha, ha."

Longarm stood. He had everything he needed in his carpetbag, which was on the steel rack overhead. His saddle and rifle were back in the baggage car, but he couldn't imagine needing either of them here in Kitts-town. He hauled the bag down onto the seat beside him, lit a slim dark cheroot from the dwindling supply in his inside coat pocket, and waited patiently for the Union Pacific conductor to return.

Hell, with no work needing to be done until he could get home to Denver, and some friends in town that he could visit with, this layover was going to be the next best thing to a vacation.

Wasn't it?

Chapter 2

"Marshal? You awake in there, Marshal? I have hot water here if you're wanting to shave yourself."

Longarm yawned and shoved the sheet and thick quilt aside, swinging his bony legs off the side of the bed and sitting up.

That, he quickly decided, was a mistake. Probably he should have stayed right where he was, chin deep in blankets, until the storm blew itself out. Which, judging from the screech and whistling beyond the hotel window, damn sure wasn't yet.

Still, awake was awake and up was up. He might as well get on with things.

"Marshal?"

"Coming." When he stood it felt like someone had glazed the floorboards with a thin layer of ice. He blinked, and with something of a start realized that the street-side wall of his room *was* iced over. A white, frosty rime of powder ice lay a quarter-inch thick on most of the wall and the window was completely opaque, buried under its own load of thick ice. No damn wonder the room felt so bone-chilling cold. The benefit of a couple of open registers to let heat rise from down-stairs wasn't anything like enough to combat the frigid wind that battered and rocked the three-story-tall build-ing.

Longarm rubbed his eyes, and out of sheer force of habit picked up his gunbelt, before unbolting the door and peeping through a narrow crack to see a pair of huge blue eyes set in a freckled, gap-tooth face. The boy was carrying a crockery pitcher from which steam drifted like smoke. Longarm grunted—he wasn't quite up to coherent speech just yet—and swung the door wide.

The grinning boy—damn anybody who could be so cheerful and bouncy on a lousy morning like this—half filled the basin on a corner stand and stepped cockily forward to accept the nickel Longarm handed him.

"Thanks, kid. How, uh, how are the meals down-stairs?"

"Best you'll find this side of Cheyenne, sir."

"Cheap?"

"A dollar."

Longarm winced. The boy grinned. "It's okay, sir. The railroad is paying for it."

"I didn't take the railroad's offer of a shared room."

"That don't make no difference, sir. You're still on the books for Union Pacific layover benefit. They'll pay your meals and sixty cents a day on your room. Mr. Wiggins has the rest of your room cost on the voucher you gave him."

"You pay a lot of attention to what's going on here," Longarm said.

The boy grinned. "My pa has a two-thirds share in this ol' hotel, Marshal. One of these days it's gonna be mine. All of it."

"Y'know, son, I believe that it will for a fact. Now

8

if you'll excuse me, I better get to my shaving before that water gets cold."

"Yes, sir. And Marshal, sir, if there's anything you need, you just ask for me. Jim Jennison Junior. You hear?"

"I do, young Jim, and I thank you."

The boy let himself out, and Longarm bolted the door closed behind him, then gave some attention to getting dressed and ready to face the day. A shave, a shit, and some groceries first, then off to visit with Clay while he waited for the track to be cleared. Could be worse.

He was not a block distant from the hotel and already Longarm's ears were deceptively numb. Dangerously numb. If he spent much time like this, he would wind up with frostbite. Damn ears would go white, then blacken with rot and fall plumb off his face. How the hell was a man supposed to keep a hat out of his eyes if he didn't have ears to prop it up on.

Not that he was wearing his hat at the moment. With a blue norther whistling down the main street of Kittstown, it would have been stupid to wear a hat. Angle your head a fraction of an inch the wrong way and a hat would soar off to Utah or some such lonesome place. Instead he'd wrapped a thin, knitted muffler around his head to try to keep the bite of the wind away. But it turned out that that covering, the best he happened to have with him, wasn't nearly enough, so he headed into the doorway of the Kittstown Mercantile.

"Mister," the proprietor greeted him, "you must be near to desperate for whatever brought you here. Personally, I only unlocked the door out of habit. And I wouldn't have come to work at all if I didn't live upstairs." The fellow was a tiny wisp of a man, probably not more than five feet and a half tall, if that, and weighing no more than a good sack of the flour he sold.

"It didn't seem so bad when I set out," Longarm admitted.

"What is it I can do you for, friend?"

"Do you happen to have any fur hats or at least some earmuffs?"

"Would some Army-issue coyote fur hats do what you want?"

"Perfect." The bulky things looked like hell, but the fur-covered earflaps would keep a mule's floppy ears warm as toast.

The storekeeper rooted through a crate and came up with one likely-looking gray-brown hat, then found an identical item under his counter. He laid the two of them side by side for Longarm's inspection. "Dollar," he said, "for this one here. Fifty cents for that one."

"Why the difference?"

The man grinned. When he did that, Longarm saw that the storekeeper wasn't nearly as old as Longarm first thought. The man's hairline had receded halfway back on his scalp so that he looked mostly bald when viewed from in front, and a set of gold-rimmed spectacles lent weight to the impression of age. At first Longarm had assumed he was in his late thirties or early forties. Now Longarm revised that estimate backward, judging the slightly built fellow to be still in his twenties. Twenty-six or -seven? About there. He seemed bright and pleasant enough, though.

"The difference is," the cheerful storekeeper said, "that both of them come out of a shipment of assorted surplus items. This fifty-cent hat, mister, is one the supplier back in Missouri claims to have treated against lice and other vermin. The dollar hat, on the other hand, is one that I personally fumigated over burning sulphur smoke. Feel free to pick and choose."

10

"Ah, yes," Longarm said with a nod. "Y'know, sir, it occurs to me that the dollar hat there is a particularly nice one. Very handsome."

"Very," the storekeeper agreed. "Shall I wrap it for you?"

"Don't bother."

"No extra charge."

"Good of you, I'm sure." Longarm untied the thongs that held the earflaps high, pulled off the useless muffler he'd wrapped around his head, then tugged the hat firmly on. He felt warmer already. "Thanks." No sense in being wasteful; since the thing happened to be handy anyway, he took the muffler and wrapped it several times around his neck, and for good measure pulled the collar of his sheepskin coat as high as it would go.

"Before you go, is there anything else I can sell you?" the storekeeper asked. "Think hard, friend. You may be the only customer I get today, and I want to make the most of you whilst you're here." The grin flashed again.

"No, there isn't, I . . . no, wait a minute there. Maybe there is something else after all. You know Clay Waring, of course. I seem to recall there was some hard candy stuff that he was fond of. Not horehound. It was, uh . . . oh, I can't call it to mind at the moment."

"Sour lemon drops," the storekeeper offered.

"That was it. Sour lemon. Let me have a little poke of those to take along. It's Clay I'm going to see today and . . ." Longarm frowned. "Did I say something wrong, mister? You look kind of . . ."

"Clay was a friend of yours, sir?"

"I would call him a friend, yes. But . . . did you say 'was'?"

"That I did. I'm sorry to convey bad news, sir, but Clay Waring is dead."

11

Chapter 3

"How?" Longarm demanded, his voice suddenly harsh. "And more to the point, what's happened to the fellow that killed Clay?"

"I know what you're thinking," the storekeeper said. "It's natural enough. A fine peace officer like Clay, you're thinking of him going down upholding the law. Or saving some child's life. Something noble and fine like that. The truth isn't near so dramatic."

Longarm raised an eyebrow and waited for the man to continue.

"About, oh, three weeks ago Clay's wife . . . do you know her?"

Longarm nodded.

"Right, well, this was on a Saturday morning, it was, and Marjorie asked Clay to help her with some work in the yard. Clay was raking leaves and piling them and some rotted manure on top of Marjorie's peony beds. He worked up a sweat doing it though it was a cold day, so he took his coat off and draped it over the fence. Later on some of the fellows walked by and stopped to chat, and Clay never thought to put the coat back on.

He stood there all wet with sweat in his shirtsleeves and talked over the fence for a spell, and then went back to his yard work. That night be caught a grippe of some kind. Took on a bad chill, of course, and woke up the next morning burning with fever and not able to get out of the bed.

"Poor soul never did get off his bed again, though Marjorie and some of us neighbors did everything any of us could think of trying to help. Hot whiskey toddies, extra blankets, hot-coal foot warmers, just everything. It didn't do Clay a lick of good. The grippe settled in his lungs and just purely filled them up. He lingered until the following Friday, and died just past dinnertime. Marjorie was with him when he went. They were holding hands. A fine couple. This community will miss Clay Waring something awful."

"I can believe that," Longarm agreed. "Helluva lousy way for a good man to go out." He sighed. "Reckon I'll have to go pay my respects to the widow."

"No need," the storekeeper told him.

"Pardon me?"

"I didn't mean there was no need exactly, but that there is no point in you going all that way in weather like this. Marjorie took Clay's body back home for burial."

"They came from someplace in Michigan, wasn't it?" Longarm asked.

"Uh, huh. Little place, to hear them tell it. Litchfield. I don't know where it is exactly. Somewhere just barely short of heaven, which seems to be about where to find most everybody's home place."

Longarm had his own opinions about that, but kept them to himself. After all, there were those who looked back on their early days with fondness. Or so he'd been told.

"To tell you the truth," the storekeeper volunteered, "I don't expect Marjorie Waring to stay once she comes back to Kittstown. My sense of it is that she will return, but probably only to close out their affairs here. I would think she will go back to her own people once things here have been taken care of."

"She came from the same little town, didn't she?" Longarm said.

The bespectacled little man nodded. "They were childhood sweethearts. Pity they never had children."

"Yes, I'm sure." Longarm had his own ideas about that too. And kept them carefully to himself. "Well, I reckon I won't be needing those sour lemon candies. Might could use some more cheroots if you have a decent make. Let me see."

"Sure thing, friend. By the way"—the fellow leaned across his counter with a hand extended—"I'm Ira Parminter. Mayor Parminter if you like." He grinned. "As of two days ago."

"Got the hang of it yet?" Longarm asked after shaking Parminter's hand and introducing himself.

"Fortunately, the job of being mayor here is more honorary in nature than it is demanding. I fully expect a quiet and uncomplicated term in office."

"And I hope for your sake that wish is fulfilled," Longarm told him. "Say, now, that pale-leaf cigar right there. Is that a box of Tio Fulvio brand? How many you got left there? I'll take ten of them, no, make that fifteen if you have enough."

Longarm completed his purchases and made his way back to the Jennison Arms, grateful for the warmth of the fur hat even for that short distance outdoors. Damn, but between the wind and the cold, it was about enough to chase a man's dauber clean out of sight. In weather like this even a stud horse would have to squat to pee.

Longarm felt considerably better once he was back in the coal-fired warmth of the hotel lobby. Now if this storm would just be nice enough to blow itself out . . .

Chapter 4

If there is one thing you can say about storms, it is that the damn things are boring. Mind-numbing. There just isn't all that much for a man to do, especially if the hotel is crowded with dozens, maybe scores, of similarly stranded travelers, practically everyone of whom is competing for the few outdated newspapers available in one small lobby.

Longarm managed to amuse himself through lunchtime, but that was about all the indoor fun he could stand for one day.

Besides, United States Marshal Billy Vail and the rest of the bunch back in Denver were no doubt finding themselves unable to proceed with the business of law enforcement without the presence of Deputy Marshal Custis Long. Yeah, he didn't doubt that for an instant. Better he should set their minds at ease and assure them he would be along as soon as God and the Union Pacific Railroad made further travel possible.

He stood and stretched, rising to his full height of six feet and then some. He wasn't especially impressed by what the others in the Jennison Arms lobby would be seeing when they looked his way. But he wasn't exactly disappointed to realize that viewers of the female persuasion generally seemed to approve of what they found in him.

The tall deputy known to his friends as Longarm was a lean, brown man. He had dark brown hair—which at the moment could use some trimming—and a huge sweep of matching brown mustache. His features were more rugged than handsome, with weather wrinkles at the corners of eyes and mouth and a permanent deep tan from spending hours and days in the saddle.

He wore black stovepipe boots, corduroy trousers, and a brown leather vest over a checked flannel shirt. A watch chain crossed his flat belly, and slightly below it was a double-action Colt revolver set in a cross-draw holster.

He shivered in anticipation of what was to come, since the hotel lobby was overly warm from a combination of well-stoked stoves and the presence of an over-abundance of warm bodies, then went upstairs to his room to retrieve his coat, gloves, and newly purchased fur hat.

Outside, the roar and tumult of windblown snow was unabated, and a thick rime of frost continued to turn the front wall of his room dead white over the bright pattern printed onto the wallpaper.

Helluva lovely day. You bet.

Longarm went downstairs and ventured out into the cold, having to do some fairly serious pushing just to get the front door open against the insistent thrust of the wind. Behind him he could sense a stir and grumble as people in the lobby were treated to a blast of frigid air.

He let the door slap closed, and bent over to force his way onto the street. Visibility was poor, but not quite impossible. He found his way to the U.P. depot and the telegraph office adjacent to it.

"Afternoon, friend. I'm glad to find you at work today," he told the telegrapher.

"You wouldn't find me here if I had any say about it." The man frowned. "This was supposed to be my day off, but the boss sent word he's sick and couldn't make it in. Huh! I know the sickness he's got. Same damn one I'd have if I was the boss and could order some poor working stiff to go out in the cold so's I wouldn't have to. But that isn't your worry, is it. So what can I do for you? The standard message that the railroad will pay for?"

"That should be good enough, I suppose."

"Just give me your name and the address you want the wire sent to. I'll take care of the rest."

"Thanks." Longarm wrote it down for him.

"If it isn't my pleasure exactly, then it's at least my job." The telegrapher smiled. "No problem, uh . . ." He peered at the paper Longarm handed him. "Marshal. You're really a U.S. marshal?"

"Just a deputy."

"Huh. That's all right. And mighty nice of you not to blame me for keeping you here."

"Oh, I would, believe me, if I thought this storm was your fault."

"Well, I appreciate your attitude, Marshal. It isn't one that all the rail passengers share."

"Been getting a hard time from some of them?" Longarm asked.

"You know how people can be. Pretty unreasonable, some of them."

"So I've heard tell," Longarm said. "Do I owe you anything for that wire, neighbor?"

"No, sir, not a thing. This first message the railroad

will pay for. Any more and the charges are up to you. Which is something not everybody seems to understand today."

"I see. Say, could I ask for your advice?"

"Stock market, politics, or questions of the heart? I have answers for all of those. And worth every penny you'd pay for them."

Longarm laughed. "Free, I take it."

"Sure, what else?"

"My question isn't so difficult. I was wondering where I might find a bottle of good rye whiskey to take back to my room. A hedge against the future, if you see what I mean."

The telegrapher smiled and nodded. He picked up a pencil and began drawing a rough sketch. "Look here now. You can't miss it."

The words struck fear deep into Longarm's heart. "You can't miss it" is one of those phrases that often presages disaster.

Still and all . . .

The Old Heidelberg Tavern was doing a bang-up business considering—or perhaps because of—the weather. The place was pretty well packed with customers, some of whom Longarm recognized from the train. There was also a sizable local crowd, identifiable by their rougher clothing and calmer demeanor.

The place was dark and humid, with sawdust on the floor and a wet-dog smell as snow melted off dozens of woolen coats in the heat given off by a pair of large, glowing potbelly stoves.

Longarm made his way to a vacant spot along the bar, and was quickly greeted by one of the two bartenders on duty at the moment.

"Howdy to you, friend. I'd like a double shot of the best rye you stock," Longarm said.

"Two bits," the bartender said by way of welcome. "In advance." So much for the notion that all Kittstown residents were warm and friendly. Longarm dug into his pocket and came up with a quarter, which he showed but did not let go of quite yet. Let the pipsqueak son-uvabitch come up with his side of the bargain. Then he could have the damn quarter.

The bartender served up a generous tot of whiskey, and Longarm released his grip on the two-bit piece. The rye, when he got around to tasting it, was as mellow and fine as the barman was sour. Longarm let the heat of the liquor spread through his belly for a moment before he poured a little more down where the first swallow had gone. The second taste was even better than the first.

"Another?" the bartender asked.

"Another," Longarm agreed. He was so pleased with the rye that this time he passed his quarter right along.

He took the second glass and turned, leaning on the bar and enjoying looking over the crowd. There were some card games in progress, and a pair of smiling whores wandered through the place flashing tits by way of advertisement.

At a table nearby there was a middle-aged woman, much too nicely dressed to be a whore herself. She had a plate of small, sugar-dusted cookies in front of her and a cup of a pale, hot beverage that Longarm guessed to be tea of some sort. If he had to guess, a woman like that, seen in a place like this, either owned the whole shebang or at least supervised the whores on somebody else's behalf. And if he had to guess, Longarm would say she probably owned the whole deal: the whiskey, the women, and a house cut of whatever gaming took place here.

She happened to be looking in his direction, so he lifted his glass in silent toast to her business skills, and was rewarded with a small smile in return.

Longarm took a small swallow of the excellent rye and went on surveying the customers. His attention was drawn back to the lady at the table a few moments later, however.

"I will thank you to leave me alone, sir." The words were polite enough, but the voice carried real venom in it. The speech was directed toward a man Longarm was pretty sure he had seen aboard the train yesterday. Of course. It was the same loudmouthed shit-for-brains who'd been arguing with the conductor about pressing forward on schedule. He hadn't grown up much overnight. But then some people never did seem to manage that most basic of human functions.

"Two dollars, honey, and you don't even have to get all the way naked," he said. "Besides, after you been with me, you'll want to pay me for the privilege." The fellow—he had to be pretty well drunk to be talking like that—decided he was mighty damn funny, and laughed so hard he should have choked. Except the lady wasn't that lucky.

"Five dollars," the man tried again, "if you suck me and my buddy over there. Five dollars, honey."

Longarm set his empty glass down and took the two strides necessary to place him at the businessman's elbow. "I think you've had about enough, Harry."

"I'm not Harry, damn it. I'm George. And who the hell are you?"

"I'm the guy who's suggesting it would be a fine idea if you was to sleep it off now. By yourself. Okay, Harry?" Longarm took a firm grip just above George's elbow, and squeezed. From a distance, the contact probably looked like a friendly little gesture, but George suddenly went pale and his knees became a mite loose and rubbery.

"Hey, mister, that—"

"Tell the lady good-bye now, Harry. It's time for you and your buddy to leave."

"Damn, I . . ."

"Say it, Harry."

"Yes, sir, I . . . I'm real sorry, lady, but my friend and I will be running along now."

"Nice to have had this chat, I'm sure," the woman said.

"Good-bye, Harry," Longarm said. "Don't get lost on your way back to the hotel now."

"Yeah, I, uh . . ."

"Harry."

"Yes, sir?"

"One thing. I notice you have a palm gun in your left-hand coat pocket. A .32 or something inoffensive like that? I want you to know, Harry, that if you even think about taking it out to admire it, I will put a .44 slug smack between your horns. Do you take my meaning, Harry?"

"I do. Yes, sir, I surely do."

"Say good-bye, George."

"Good-bye, ma'am."

The businessman, still pale and shaken, whispered something to his pal, and the two of them hurried out of the Old Heidelberg with their tails between their legs. More or less.

Longarm tried to tip his hat to the woman, and realized too late that he had on the fluffy fur thing instead of his own good Stetson. He wound up feeling more foolish than gallant.

"My apologies, ma'am. Good old Harry there is even worse when he's sober." He touched the front of his

22

hat, deliberately this time, smiled, and turned back to find his whiskey glass gone and someone else standing where Longarm had been. Oh, well. Some days are just like that.

Chapter 5

While Longarm was still trying to decide if he should beg the surly bartender for another rye or strike out into the chilly arms of the snowstorm, the barman turned, suddenly friendly. The fellow came up with a fresh bottle of rye, seal still unbroken, and served up both a smile—well, a showing of teeth that Longarm was pretty sure was supposed to be a smile—and half a water tumbler of what proved to be an exceptionally fine rye whiskey.

"What's this . . . ?" Before Longarm could complete the question the bartender was nodding in the direction of the table where the nice-looking lady sat nursing her cookies and tea. She motioned for Longarm to come over. He noticed that the invitation apparently did not seem to include his actually joining her at the table. But she did want him to come stand closer. What the hell. He took his drink—it was the best whiskey he'd had in months or maybe longer—and wandered over there. "Ma'am." He nodded.

"I haven't thanked you properly," she said.

Longarm looked at his glass and grinned. "Mighty

good way to say thank you to *my* mind, ma'am."

"Good." She smiled. "My name is Amanda Forsyth. And you are?"

"Custis Long, Miss Forsyth. Of Denver."

The smile flashed again. "Oh yes. The deputy United States marshal who's staying at the Jennison Arms."

"I see you stay well informed, Miss Forsyth."

"Forewarned, sir, is forearmed. And for the record, it is Mrs. Forsyth, not Miss."

"My apologies for the error, ma'am."

"Is there anything I can do for you, Marshal Long? A tumble with one of my doxies, perhaps? Pick any girl in the place. No charge."

"You're very generous, Mrs. Forsyth."

"Not at all, Marshal. Merely appreciative."

"Thanks, but I'm content with this for the time being." He took a small sip from the hefty slug that had been poured for him.

"If you change your mind . . ."

"I'll let you know. Thanks."

Amanda Forsyth shrugged and turned her attention back to her cookies and tea.

Longarm turned to go, but was stopped by a young cowboy who wore a six-gun tied low on his leg in the best of fast-draw fashion. The youngster tapped Longarm on the elbow, and Longarm hoped the boy wasn't some half-drunk idiot wanting to make a reputation by gunning down a lawman.

"Yeah?"

"You're the deputy they call Longarm, aren't you, sir?"

Sir. Not many said sir when they were wanting to pick a fight. But then, there could be a first time for damn near anything, Longarm supposed.

"My friends call me Longarm, that's true enough," Longarm admitted.

"My buddies and me, Mr. Longarm, we'd be real tickled if you'd sit in and play a few hands of poker with us. Low stakes is all we can afford, though. If you don't have anything better to do, sir." The cowboy grinned. "We'd be real honored if you would join us, sir."

Making a gunman's reputation? Not hardly. Longarm felt purely ashamed of himself. "Why, I'd be pleased to sit in for a few hands, son. Now tell me about yourself if you wouldn't mind, and let me meet those friends of yours too."

The youngster led the way through the busy tables at the Old Heidelberg. The boys—it turned out there were four of them—all liked to play simple draw poker. And were in serious need of instruction as to the finer points of the game, instruction which Longarm was pleased to provide. At their expense, of course.

Billy Madlock, Jason Tyler, Ronnie Gordon, and Carl Benson were young, happy-go-lucky, and easy to get along with. All four worked for a cow and calf outfit north of Kittstown. All four, naturally enough, were out of work for the winter. That was the usual pattern among the type. They had work from the first grass of spring through the fall's final gather and shipment of the calf crop. After that, they lived off whatever money they'd managed to save—which didn't generally amount to a hell of a lot—and whatever few dollars they could pick up here and there in town. Which mostly meant they lived free and easy during the summer months and hand-to-mouth the rest of the time. If it bothered this bunch, they sure managed to avoid showing it. Longarm found them to be good, if a mite enthusiastic, company.

"Tell us about your most famous cases," they pressed him.

"Who're you here to arrest this trip, sir?"

"Do you need four extra deputies to cover your back, Longarm? We'd work cheap. Ow, quit kicking me, Ronnie. Longarm knows I didn't mean that. Hey, we'd work for nothing, you know that? It'd be a kick to tell the boys come summer that we helped the real live Longarm on a case."

"So who are you here to arrest, sir? I mean, I know it's supposed to be a secret and all. But you can tell us. We won't repeat it anywhere. Honest."

They seemed purely disappointed when Longarm insisted that he was only in town because of the Union Pacific weather layover.

"You aren't funning us about that, are you? We'd help you, Marshal. Truly we would, and proud to do it."

"Thanks, but I really don't have a case here. Just a stopover until the tracks are clear."

Jason and Carl sighed with disappointment, and Billy looked so sad he reminded Longarm of a red tick pup that had its mother's teat taken away. "Sorry, fellows, but I can't make up something that isn't so just for your amusement."

"No, sir, I suppose not. And I reckon I'll see your bet, sir, and raise you three cents."

"Call."

"I'm out."

"I'll see that. Sir?"

"Oh, I'll stay, I reckon."

It was a slow, undemanding sort of game. Just the sort of thing to pass some time while the wind howled the windowpanes loose in their frames and the snow piled deep in the drifts.

The only thing Longarm worried about was that he

might take too much money off these youngsters. He suspected they could ill afford to have any of their money leave the foursome, so after a few hands he backed off and made a point not to stay in the pots that looked to get serious. Although it hurt like hell to toss in three kings without so much as a draw.

Still, he was damned lucky. Small though it was, he had himself a paycheck through the winter. These boys and thousands more just like them scattered from Montana right on down to Texas weren't so fortunate.

"Bartender," he called at one point. "Bring us a bottle here and some fresh glasses. On my tab if you please."

Amanda Forsyth's generosity covered the use of a whore if he wanted, but apparently did not extend to free liquor by the bottle. Which was fair enough, of course. The whiskey had to be paid for by the handsome proprietress. A whore's time did not.

Longarm paid for the bottle, and cut the deck of freshly shuffled cards that Billy offered.

All in all, he thought, he'd spent worse afternoons.

Chapter 6

Longarm slept in late. The heck with young entrepreneur Jim Jennison Junior and his hot shaving water. It was just too damn cold to crawl out from under the covers before, say, noon.

When he did wake up to stay—closer to eight of the clock, actually, than to the magical twelve—he decided it really was a shame he couldn't sleep any more. Because there certainly wasn't anything in or about Kittstown worth getting up for.

The outside wall of his room was still coated thick with a rime of frost, and his window was still entirely opaque. Outside, he could still hear the wind moaning and thrashing and battering at the walls. Longarm suspected there wasn't much point in asking if the railroad track was clear yet. With wind like that to contend with, a plow would be lucky to clear its own length. Any hole punched through the drifts would likely close in immediately behind the coal car as fresh drifts formed where the old ones used to be.

It was a pity. Kittstown, Wyoming, was no doubt a nice enough place. But Denver was a helluva lot more amusing, good weather or bad.

Still, a man was best off if he was willing to put up with what he had and never mind the wishes and the what-ifs.

Longarm sat up, scratched an itch in his armpit, and headed for the thunder mug. No way in hell was he going out to the backhouse for his morning dump. Not in that wind, he wasn't.

He shaved—in cold water, thank you—and just to insure that he looked and felt mostly human, made it a point to put on a tie that was clean and nicely knotted. That done, he went downstairs to breakfast.

He was almost done with a plate of ham and fried potatoes—no eggs were available thanks to the storm and the inconvenience of not having a delivery of produce and other such perishables for several days running—when the Jennison boy came trotting into the dining room and headed straight for Longarm in a colt-ish lope. The boy was muffled and bundled to the ear-lobes, and carried a peck of snow with him when he came.

"Marshal, sir. The mayor wants you to come, sir. Quick."

"You know what for, son?"

"No, sir, but he wants you. He told me to fetch you right away."

"At his store?"

"Yes, sir. Right away quick."

Longarm grunted and gave a rueful look toward the remaining ham on his plate. But if he was needed . . . He wrapped the rest of the ham inside a slice of bread, and munched on it as he went up to his room to get his coat and fur cap. Then he came back downstairs and out into the cutting chill of the wind.

If anything, it was colder and snowier today than it had been to begin with.

He turned his face away from the freezing cold and hunched his shoulders. Damn, but it was nasty out.

"I'd like you to come with me, Marshal. I, um, may need some advice," Ira Parminter told him when Longarm stepped inside the mayor's store.

"Something wrong?"

Parminter motioned toward a trio of children, boys about ten or eleven years old, Longarm guessed. All three of them looked unnaturally pale, and there was frozen puke decorating the woolen coat of one of the boys. "This is Marshal Long, Jacky," Parminter said. "I want you to tell him what you boys told me."

The tallest and apparently oldest of the three gave Longarm a skeptical look and then shrugged. "Me and Bert and Bennie there was playing. We was playing hide-and-seek. You know?"

Longarm nodded.

"Yeah, well, there aren't so many places you can hide when it's like this, but while we was out . . . our folks thought we was at each other's houses, you know?"

"I know how that is," Longarm assured the boy.

"Right. So we was out. And we thought we'd just, well . . ."

"What Jacky is avoiding getting around to, Longarm, is that the boys broke into Old Man Travis's shack," Parminter said.

"Old Man Travis?"

"That's what they call Darby Travis. Darby is about three days older than dirt. A harmless enough old codger. He has a cabin on the outskirts of town where he lives by himself. Every once in a while he disappears. Stays gone for a few weeks, sometimes for several months at a time, then some morning there he'll be again."

"Uh, huh. I take it he's been away lately?" Longarm said.

"That's right. And the boys, of course, knew he couldn't come back until the tracks are open again so they would be safe if they wanted to break into his place."

"Bust it up?" Longarm asked. "Dump all his flour and sugar and stuff on the floor? Fun stuff like that?"

Jacky shook his head. "We didn't want to hurt nothing, sir. Honest. We just wanted to . . . like . . . look around a little."

"Go on."

"Yeah, so anyway, we busted the hasp on the door lock. Bert found this prybar in the shed, see, and we used that to pop the lock open. And we went in and it was all cold and quiet and kinda dark in there, and we started telling ghost stories and making spooky sounds. You know?"

"Sure, kid. Go on."

"Yeah, well, it was all kinda funny. And then Bert found a lantern an' some matches an' he lit the lantern, and Bennie got the giggles and he sat down on the side of Old Man Travis's bed, and then Bert screamed and Bennie thought he was just being funny. But he turned and looked and right there, Marshal, right there in front of his face an' staring right at him, right there in the old man's bed was this . . . this *dead* person. You know?"

But this time Longarm did not know. "A dead person? You're sure about that?"

Bennie, Longarm took it, was the boy with the puke all over him. No wonder.

"We're sure, sir. Honest we are."

"The dead person was Mr. Travis?" Longarm asked.

"No, sir. This dead person is a girl, sir."

"We don't know who," the one called Bert said.

"We never seen her before."

"I seen her once. At least I think it was her."

"That's enough," boys, Parminter said. "You did the right thing coming here and telling me about it."

"You won't . . . I mean . . . you won't tell our folks about us being in Old Man Travis's place, will you, sir?" Jacky asked in a voice that had much too much feigned innocence in it.

"I won't make you any promises about that," Parminter told them. Longarm liked that about the young mayor. A man who would lie to a kid would lie to a grown-up just as readily. If perhaps with a little more care as to how he went about it.

The mayor turned to Longarm. "I don't know anything about this sort of thing, Marshal, and with Clay gone . . . I was hoping you would come with me. In case there has to be an investigation or whatever. I mean, it could be a case of death by natural causes. But we don't know that yet. Do we?"

Parminter looked considerably relieved when Longarm assured him that he would go along with the mayor and take a look at this alleged dead body that the boys claimed to have found.

Chapter 7

The only creature on earth that would even consider going all the way out to a stupid empty damn cabin in weather this terrible, Longarm decided, was an energetic ten-year-old boy.

Darby Travis's place was more than a quarter mile past the edge of town, upstream along a tiny willow-lined rill not deep enough to keep a frog damp. Most of the year the path running along the west side of the creek—locally and unofficially known as Travis's Trickle—likely offered a pleasant little stroll. At the moment, however, it threatened life and limb. Literally. If it hadn't been for the line of snow-plastered crack-willows, they would surely have lost their way. As it was, Longarm hoped the mayor damn sure knew where they were going because one moment of confusion could have downright serious consequences.

When the path took them into the lee of a grove of runty, twisted little cottonwoods, however, Parminter grabbed Longarm by the elbow and guided him into a massive snowdrift.

At least the big white heap looked like nothing more

than an unusually large drift. What it turned out to be was Old Man Travis's cabin, its twisted, mud-chinked logs hidden behind a wall of wind-piled snow.

The door, broken lock dangling, stood open, and the interior looked as cold and empty as a tomb.

Which under the circumstances was not at all unreasonable, Longarm thought.

"See anything?" he asked.

Parminter shook his head. "I thought those kids said they lighted a lantern in here."

"There." Longarm pointed. The lantern, its globe broken, lay on the floor close to the open door. It was plain damn lucky that the thing hadn't set the cabin afire when it was dropped.

Parminter, still in the lead, picked the lantern up and shook it. Satisfied that there was still oil in it, he stepped deeper inside the shack to be out of the swirling wind coming through the doorway and struck a match. As soon as the lantern was lighted, Longarm pulled the door closed behind him. There was no change in temperature, of course, but shutting away the sound of the wind made it seem somehow warmer and more comfortable.

"Well, the boys weren't lying," Longarm said while the mayor was still busy adjusting the lantern wick.

"Pardon me?"

Longarm pointed. Travis's cot was a crude affair, made of split aspen logs pegged into a corner so as to provide solid support on two sides, and with a chunk of tree section acting as a leg at the foot of the narrow bunk. At first glance the bed simply looked untidy and rumpled. But closer inspection disclosed an unnaturally pale hand exposed beneath a fold of twisted quilt and a shadowed cheek barely visible at the pillow end of the bed. "Bring that light closer, will you?" Longarm asked.

He moved in front of the mayor and went to the bed. Yeah, the boys were right all right. Longarm pulled the covers back out of the way so he could get a better look.

The body was that of a young woman. Naked. Very badly battered. The right side of her face was distorted with swelling and discoloration, to the point that even someone who knew her would have had difficulty trying to recognize her. There were no visible stab or gunshot wounds. At least none that Longarm could see as she was now positioned, lying face-up on the old man's dirty bunk with her hands—oddly, Longarm thought—arranged across her stomach in a common burial posture.

She'd had a fine figure, he saw. Her breasts were of something better than average size, and were pink-tipped and exceptionally firm. Or would have been in life, that is. They were damn well solid, of course, now that she was frozen.

Which, Longarm realized, was something of an assumption based on the near-white pallor caused by the cold. He really had no way to judge how long she'd been dead or the condition of her flesh just by looking. So he touched her.

He prodded the slight swell of her lower belly with a rigid fingertip, encountering more than a little resistance. He pushed harder, and was able to feel some small amount of give, the flesh over her stomach acting as a solidly frozen bridge or ceiling on the relatively empty cavity inside. Longarm grunted.

"What?" Parminter asked.

"Takes a helluva time for a body to freeze," Longarm ventured. "There's heat built up inside. I dunno why. That's why you have to gut a deer or elk if you don't want the meat to spoil. It don't seem to matter how cold it is, the heat stays inside unless you let the cold get in. She's been dead"—he shrugged—"couple days anyhow. Could be even longer. I can't say for certain sure."

"A week, do you think?"

"Could be, I suppose," Longarm agreed, although with certain reservations in his own mind.

"The last I recall seeing Darby Travis was just about a week ago," the mayor said.

"You figure he killed the girl for some reason and then ran?"

"It's a reasonable assumption."

"This Travis fella, he wouldn't be smart enough to move the body elsewhere so it wouldn't be found in his own bed?"

"Not if he panicked. I mean, it looks pretty much an open-and-shut case, doesn't it? The girl is here in Darby's own bed. And he left town without warning."

Longarm grunted again. Whatever the facts, they weren't his to worry about. Killing people, even young and pretty girls, was not a violation of federal law. A deputy U.S. marshal had no jurisdiction over local affairs in Kittstown, Wyoming.

On a whim, though, Longarm took the lantern from the mayor and held it closer to the corpse, moving it up and down, back and forth, so as to give light from different angles.

"Why are you doing that?" Parminter asked.

Longarm explained.

"And do you see anything?"

Longarm nodded, pointing. "See there?"

"No." The mayor leaned closer to scrutinize the curling brown patch of scanty pubic hair.

Longarm moved the lantern a little. "Now?" Longarm prompted. "Not high up in the hair. Down around the pussy and on the skin of her thighs way up high. Now do you see?"

"It looks sort of . . . shiny," Parminter said.

"Exactly," Longarm said. "Know what that is?"

The mayor shook his head.

"Dried come. It's always shiny like that when it dries on. Helluva lot of it too, in the hair and on her legs." He moved the lantern and looked closer. "Down here lower on her left leg too. She dripped some. That means she was standing up at one point after she was fucked. And look here." Longarm dug a fingertip through the screen of dark hair low on the dead girl's mound. "There more has leaked out and trickled down onto her butthole. I'd say she got it again while she was laying down and never had a chance to get up again. She was killed after that time." He looked at Parminter. "How old did you say this Travis is?"

The mayor shrugged. "I don't know. Pretty old."

"You think he could get it up twice in a row like that?"

"Like what? He could have kept her captive for days before he killed her," Parminter countered.

Longarm frowned, considering. "You're right. I reckon he could at that."

Parminter managed a weak smile. "Besides, I wouldn't think age should keep a man down. Personally, I intend to still be getting it on a regular basis when I'm ninety."

"And I hope you do at that." Longarm looked the girl's body over again, and shrugged again. "You haven't said if you recognize her."

"I . . . think maybe."

"Maybe? Mr. Mayor, pardon me for pointing out the obvious, but Kittstown ain't so awful big that you should have trouble keeping track of who-all lives here." In an effort to help, Longarm took hold of the girl's shoulder and rolled the body onto its side so Parminter could get a look at the relatively undamaged side of her face.

God, she'd been pretty, Longarm saw now. And younger than he'd thought. Fifteen or sixteen, he guessed. With a glossy spill of gleaming chestnut-colored hair puffed loose around her head and her eyes closed as if in sleep. It occurred to Longarm for the second time that after battering the girl to death, the killer had bothered to arrange the body with some care, folding the hands, closing the eyes, doing those small services that one did to prepare the dead. But not, of course, washing her, or they never would have seen the semen dried on her flesh. Damned interesting, he thought.

"I think . . . I'm pretty sure I know who she was," Parminter said finally.

"Yeah?"

"She was . . . I believe she was one of Norma Brantley's girls."

"And that would be?"

"A trollop. One of the girls working in the local whorehouse," Parminter explained. "I don't know her name, but I believe I saw her there a couple weeks ago. Just a glimpse. I could be wrong."

"Yeah, well, it's one of the hazards of the occupation, isn't it. Guy gets a little too vigorous when he's beating up on a whore, sometimes they go under. No real harm done, the way most see it. Just some hooker. Not like a real person's been harmed." Longarm scowled. "I don't think I ever heard of anybody getting any serious punishment for killing a whore. You know?"

The mayor looked away, either no longer interested or perhaps mildly embarrassed to have been able to recognize the dead girl.

Hell, the case was as good as closed already, Longarm figured. Eventually old Darby Travis would come home. If and when he did, someone might go to the trouble of

39

asking him about the girl who'd been found dead in his cabin. Or then again, no one might bother with useless questions. Easier yet, Travis wouldn't bother coming back, and pretty soon the whole thing would be forgotten and done with. It seemed a shitty fate for what had been a pretty girl.

But it wasn't Longarm's business.

He let go of the girl's shoulder, allowing the body to roll onto its back again.

When he did that he caught a momentary glimpse of something shining on the cold, pale left-side cheek.

The tiny, gleaming spot caught the light and reflected it back like a diamond chip. It didn't seem . . .

Longarm tugged the body toward him again and held the lantern close. There. On the cheek. And there again frozen on a curling eyelash.

Tears.

The girl was crying when she died. Alone. Unwanted. Undefended. Garbage in human form. But so young and so pretty and crying as she died.

Something about that reached inside Longarm's belly and twisted his gut in knots.

Something about the tears frozen onto her cheek touched him and made him want to make whoever killed this girl—barely more than a child, she'd been—understand the waste of it, make the son of a bitch know the pain and the despair and the ugliness of her death.

Not that he could take a hand in it, of course. This death was not his case to look into. The jurisdiction was strictly local.

Of course it was.

"Reckon we can go now," Longarm suggested.

"What about . . . ?" The mayor motioned weakly toward the naked corpse lying on Old Man Travis's bed.

"She'll keep. Till the spring thaw anyhow." Longarm

arranged the bedclothes to cover the girl's slim body, pausing for only a moment to peer at what should have been a serene and lovely face. Then he turned, brisk and frowning. "Let's get the hell outa here, Mr. Mayor."

Chapter 8

The trip from the Travis cabin back to Kittstown was even colder and more miserable than the walk out had been. But then Longarm and Parminter had been away from heat for a much longer period now, and were thoroughly chilled even before they set out. By the time they reached the warmth and the shelter of Parminter's store, Longarm was fairly sure his nose hairs were so brittle they were fixing to break off. The tips of his fingers stung as if they were afire—an odd sort of reaction to the cold but a common one—and his ears were completely numb.

Parminter shed his coat with a grunt of anticipation and said, "I have some brandy behind the counter, and personally I intend to have a slug of it. Sort of put some heat in my belly. Care to join me?"

Brandy wasn't Longarm's normal tipple of choice. But there were times when a departure from the norm could seem a right splendid idea. "I'd be grateful."

The mayor produced a bottle that was dusty with age and handed it over. Longarm removed the cork and took a long pull at the slightly sweet contents. The flavor was nothing he would want to repeat, but the warmth that flowed through his stomach was more than welcome. "Damn, but that's better. Thanks."

He handed the bottle back to the mayor, who helped himself to a drink and offered, "Another?"

Longarm shook his head. "No, that's enough to light the fires but not so much as to effect the judgment. Look, would you mind if I tagged along when you go talk to Norma Brantley?"

Parminter looked puzzled. "Why would I want to talk to Norma?"

"Sorry," Longarm quickly apologized. "I kinda thought you'd be wanting to look into that girl's murder."

"Murder is a very serious word, Longarm. And you said it yourself. The girl was a whore. It isn't like a regular citizen was killed."

"If you don't want to call it murder, then how 'bout manslaughter? That's a perfectly good legal charge in this territory. And there's not even the possibility of a hanging sentence to upset the voters. You could charge the mur—I mean the killer—you could charge the killer with manslaughter."

"It could have been accidental," Parminter suggested. "Don't you think?"

"No, sir, fact is I don't think even a high-priced lawyer would have balls enough to pretend that was accidental. Oh, the dying might've been accident enough. Could be whoever killed her didn't especially want for it to go that far. But the beating, Mr. Mayor, that wasn't no accident. That was cold and cruel and deliberate as a man taking a fence post to the side of his mule's head. No, whoever killed that girl beat up on her a-purpose, whether he figured for her to die or not. And I tell you the truth, sir. I'd kinda like to talk to that fella and ask

43

him just how this thing happened and what it was that he intended."

"As I understand it, Longarm, as a deputy U.S. marshal you only have authority here if competent local authority asks for your help. Is that correct?"

"Yes, sir, it is."

"And with Clay Waring dead and gone, well, I think I am probably the only local official capable of inviting your, um, assistance."

"Which of course you ain't done."

"Which I have not done," Parminter agreed, "and which I do not intend to do. And before you make any assumptions, Deputy, it is not a question of who votes or who does not. It is a matter of what I honestly feel is best for this community. I simply do not believe that the distress of accusations and murder charges and the like . . . well, I just do not think that could accomplish any worthwhile purpose."

"It could bring a murderer to justice," Longarm said softly.

"You are entitled to your beliefs, sir. I am equally entitled to mine. As it happens, I do not want to, as they say, rock the boat."

Longarm shrugged. And began buttoning his coat. "That's your decision to make, Mr. Mayor. I won't try and deny it."

"Thank you."

"If you do happen to need my help . . ."

"I know where to find you, thanks."

Longarm turned his collar high and tugged the fur hat snug, then let himself out into the wrath of the snow and icy wind.

44

Chapter 9

Longarm was in one sonuvabitch of a mood when he left the mayor's store. He felt frustrated. Useless. Dammit, if a lawman couldn't tend to the law, what the hell good was he? For that matter, what the hell good was the law if nobody wanted to bother tending to it? Walking away from that girl's murder—and murder it damn sure was, regardless of how Parminter wanted to skew his view of things—churned Longarm's gut into sour knots.

He was halfway back to the hotel when he changed his mind about his destination, and headed instead for the Old Heidelberg. The barman there remembered him. "Rye whiskey is it, Marshal?"

"Later," Longarm told him. "I'll be back for a drink later on. Right now I could use some directions."

"Anything to help," the bartender offered. "Where d'you want to go?"

"A place run by a woman name of Norma Brantley," Longarm said.

The barman frowned.

"I know Miss Forsyth has her own, uh, competing

45

business to think about," Longarm said. "But it isn't a roll in the hay that I'm looking for. Just information."

The bartender's expression softened. A little anyway. "I don't know that she'll be open for business this early."

"I told you, friend, it isn't business that I have in mind. Not that sort anyhow."

"Yeah, well, all right then." The barman used his fingertip dipped in some recently spilled liquor to sketch a crude map on the bar surface. "You can't miss it," he concluded, prompting Longarm to wonder if there was some rule written down somewhere that required all persons engaged in giving directions to conclude with that oh-so-inaccurate assurance.

"Thanks," Longarm said. "You been a big help."

"Any time."

Longarm turned and touched the front of his cap first to Miss Forsyth, who was seated demurely at a table in a far corner, and again to the friendly cowboys he'd played poker with earlier. Come evening, he thought, he just might return for that glass of rye and another round of cards.

Longarm had a bit of trouble locating Norma Brantley's whorehouse from the Old Heidelberg bartender's directions, but he chalked that up to the low visibility rather than to any chance that he could somehow "miss it." After all, it wouldn't have been possible for him to miss it. He had that on reliable authority.

As it was, he crossed the tracks just east of the railroad depot, skirted the fringes of the livestock loading chutes and acres of holding pens, picked his way through a warren of frigid, litter-strewn alleys, and found his way eventually to what was essentially a collection of tumbledown shacks tied more or less together beneath a common roof. Miz Brantley's hog ranch seemed not to have been planned but just sort of to have grown. Like a rather noxious mushroom.

Longarm investigated several of the niches and crannies along the front of the place until he decided on one that looked like an entryway. As he came nearer he could hear the bright, brittle tinkle of a cheap piano leaking through the walls. Apparently the barman had been wrong about one thing. Probably because of the storm keeping everyone indoors and mostly bored, the refuge of soiled doves was not only open, it was doing a land-rush business.

Longarm didn't bother knocking. Hell, he wouldn't have been heard over all that din going on inside anyhow. He found the latch and let himself in, stepping out of the sting of the wind and into the steamy, perfume-saturated heat of a very crowded parlor.

"Welcome, friend," a painted and grinning whore screamed in the general direction of his ear. "Take a number, mister, the wait won't be very long. Drinks over there. Billiards down that way. Relax and enjoy yourself. Your number will be called just as soon as there's a room and a girl available for your pleasure."

Take a number and wait in line. Romantic as all billy hell, Longarm figured.

But time-consuming.

He pulled out his wallet—

"No, put that away, friend. You don't need to pay till you get to the room."

—and flipped it open to expose his badge. "I'd like to have a visit with Miz Brantley, miss."

The girl—woman, actually; she was a decade or more past being called a girl even by charitable souls—went a little wide in the eyes and pale in the cheeks and began to stammer something incomprehensible.

47

"It's all right, miss. I'm not here to cause any trouble. I just wanta talk to Miz Brantley."

"Wait right here, sir. I won't be but five seconds. I promise." And she fled like a young doe getting the hell out of the cornfield once the farmers commenced shooting.

Chapter 10

The girl wasn't all that far off in her time estimate. More than five seconds, it was true, but not by so much that Longarm could find serious fault with her. Especially since when she did come back she brought in tow a matron who must surely be the inestimable proprietress of the establishment.

Norma Brantley moved through the crowd with all the steady aplomb of a sternwheeler making passage on the Mississippi. This was one *big* woman. Damned near as tall as Deputy United States Marshal Curtis Long. And outweighed him by, he guessed, a solid eighty or more pounds.

She looked fit to wrestle a bear or fistfight a lumberjack. And had the mustache to lend credence to that image. It was not, however, as handsome a one as Longarm's. He definitely gave himself the edge in that category.

She had hair the color of bright polished steel plating, applied her powder and rouge with a trowel, and had a jaw so massive she was probably capable of biting railroad spikes in two whenever she felt the yen for a toothpick. Beautiful this woman was not. But formidable? Damn, he reckoned so.

Ever mindful of etiquette, Longarm swept his hat off and made a small bow to the, um, lady. "Miz Brantley, allow me to introduce myself. I'm—"

"Damn it!" The voice, decidedly masculine, was somewhere between a bellow and a roar. It came from down one of the several hallways that branched off the central foyer where Longarm was trying to make himself known to Norma Brantley.

"Bitch!" the voice roared again. Immediately following that pronouncement there was the sharp crack of an open hand striking flesh and a piercing, and this time feminine, shriek.

The Brantley woman's attention was distracted by the interruption. Understandably.

She turned, and no doubt would have set sail in that direction except there was no need. A man appeared at the entry to the hall, clad only in a shirt, gartered stockings, and shoes. Longarm could not decide if that was an oversight, forgotten in the heat of the moment, or if the fellow simply didn't give a damn who was treated to the sight of his privates. But then maybe he thought the vision was one of inspiration, Longarm realized half a second later upon recognizing the chap. It was George of the loud mouth and ready complaint, the same sweet soul who thought himself a gift to all the world and to its womenfolk in particular.

"Are you the madam here? Well, don't just stand there. Are you? Of course you are. Do you want to beat this useless bitch or do I have to do it for you? Don't you teach these whores anything? Mind your manners, woman, or I shall have the law after you. Taking money under false pretenses. That's robbery, you know."

" 'Lissa robbed you, mister?" Brantley asked as soon as she could get a word in.

"As good as. Miserable little bitch won't do what I paid her for."

"Ma'am, that isn't so, ma'am, I swear. He only paid me two dollars, then when I got my bloomers down he said he wanted to put it up my bum. I don't do that, ma'am. That hurts terrible. Not for no lousy two dollars I don't take it in me backside, no, ma'am."

"The regular price oughta be but a dollar. Anywhere in this country a man can get laid for a dollar," good old George grumbled. "Two is twice what it ought to be to begin with. For that much I'm entitled to stick it wherever I damn please."

"I think, mister, you've already had all the fun your two dollars is going to buy you. Get out of my place. Right now."

"The hell I will." George stormed forward in the direction of the madam. The whore he'd been with grabbed for his arm, which only earned her a backhanded swat that split her lower lip and sent a spill of bright blood streaming off her chin and down her scrawny neck.

George, in the meantime, seemed fully determined to whack Brantley next. He pulled a fist back and set himself to launch it.

To Longarm that seemed rather rude behavior for a guest. Never mind that they happened to be in a whorehouse. George was nonetheless a guest. And was acting like something of an ass, which seemed to be his own unique personal style.

Longarm had been drifting along behind Brantley, listening in with roughly equal parts of curiosity and disdain. After all, he already knew that friend George was a walking, talking asshole. And Longarm more or less

51

expected this sort of behavior from the fellow.

When George decided to punch Norma Brantley, Longarm decided it was time for him to take a hand.

George threw what he no doubt believed was a wicked right, but he wasn't half quick enough. Longarm stepped in front of the madam and knocked George's blow aside with a sweep of his forearm.

Longarm grinned into the man's teeth. "Afternoon, Harry. Nice to see you again."

"You son of a bitch."

"Y'know, Harry, you really oughta be careful who you say a thing like that to." Longarm punctuated his opinion with a short little left-handed body shot so quick and unobtrusive it was likely no one else so much as saw it. George, on the other hand, felt it. There wasn't much question about that for it sank wrist-deep into the man's belly. His jaw dropped open and his complexion turned a mild and rather pleasant shade of green.

Longarm was not sure what, if anything, George might have done next. Before that could be determined, the resident bouncers had time to respond to the commotion. Three of them, each big enough to yoke, surrounded the combatants and put sure-handed come-along holds on George, on Longarm, and just to be sure, Longarm supposed, on the bleeding girl too. Since they didn't yet really know what the hell was happening, Longarm gathered, their method was simply to grab the whole damn flock all together and start tossing out everyone.

"That one," Brantley said, pointing at George. "Out."

"Yes'm," the biggest bouncer said. His voice sounded something like what Longarm imagined would be the sound of a volcano beginning to erupt. "What about his pants, ma'am? He ain't wearing no pants."

"Out," Brantley repeated.

52

The big man picked George up with no visible effort whatsoever and started off down the hall with him under one arm, George's naked, hairy ass bobbing in rhythm with his captor's stride.

"Not this one," Brantley said, and Longarm found himself back on his own two feet, hardly the worse for wear.

"And you,'Lissa. Clean yourself up and get back to work."

"Yes, ma'am." The whore turned to leave.

" 'Lissa," Brantley said in a surprisingly soft tone.

"Yes, ma'am?"

"I don't want to have any more complaints, dear, about you saying no to a gentleman."

"Yes, ma'am, but—"

"Ah!" Brantley held a finger up to caution the girl. "When the situation arises again, dear, you may explain that some services cost extra. But don't you ever tell a gentleman you won't please him. You know what will happen if that ever happens again." 'Lissa turned the same approximate shade of green that George had when Longarm sank a fist in his belly. The gentle Miz Brantley, it seemed, ran an exceptionally taut ship here.

"Thank you, boys. I don't think I will be needing you any more."

The two remaining mountain-sized lads wandered off into the shadows—which was where Longarm would just as soon they stayed; damn but they were big and quick and mighty efficient at what they did—and the madam turned her attentions finally to Longarm.

"All right, goddammit, let me see your warrant."

It's always nice to feel welcome, Longarm thought.

Chapter 11

"Either show me a warrant or get your ass outa here," the big madam demanded. She acted more pissed off with Longarm than she had with old George, he thought. Which hardly seemed reasonable.

But then who the hell ever said that people were supposed to be reasonable. No peace officer would ever make such a stupid claim, that was for sure.

"No warrant," he said, "and nothing official." He paused for half a heartbeat. "Yet. Right now all I'm asking for is a few minutes of conversation. I doubt it will ever have to go any further than that."

"I told you, bub. If you don't have a warrant you got no business here."

Longarm sighed. Loudly. He tried to look sad, resigned. "Whatever you say, ma'am." Then, brightening, he looked around and smiled just a little. "Y'know what I bet? I bet your clientele here has included some good ol' boys who're wanted by the federal court down in Denver. Yes'm, I could almost swear from some of the descriptions I've heard that you've harbored that gang of mail thieves that hit the Denver and Rio Grande express cars last month and—what was it? Last August? Something like that. I expect Judge Franklin could be talked into giving me a warrant based on that suspicion. And if he does, well, I reckon I might hafta put a seal on the doors and impound your records, bank statements, all the stuff like that. I dunno, lady, we could be onta something good here. A mite hard on you and your people, of course. But don't you worry. I know you can afford a good lawyer. Give him six, eight months to work with and he'll get all your stuff released by the court again. Unless we find something in the evidence we collect. What the hell. Let's go ahead and give it a shot.''

"Wait. You said . . . federal?'' The woman looked worried. Longarm couldn't hardly figure out why. You bet.

"That's right.''

"You aren't from Cheyenne?''

"Me? No, ma'am.'' Longarm introduced himself, this time managing to complete the task.

"I thought . . . Jessie only said you were the law. I suppose . . . I assumed . . .''

Longarm understood what the problem was. Locally, and apparently at the state level too, this woman obviously had enough pull, somehow, somewhere, that she could safely ignore most attempts at official interference. But she wouldn't have a damn speck of leverage when it came to United States Marshal William Vail. Nor, for that matter, to anyone else in the federal court system or the Attorney General's office. The federal boys in this neck of the woods—barring the odd congressman here and there and an occasional lunatic senator, and none of them counted anyway—were as honest as they come.

"You say you only want to talk a little?'' Brantley asked.

"That's right."

"Follow me."

The office was small, bare, and about as attractive as the woman who occupied it. Longarm was shown a straight-backed wooden chair with a wicker seat that needed replacing. One thing he was sure of. The profits from this business weren't being squandered on luxury appointments for the madam.

"You want a drink, Marshal?"

"No, thanks." He would have liked a rye whiskey well enough, but this was not a person he wanted to be beholden to. Not even in the smallest of ways. "Mind if I smoke?" he asked.

"Go ahead."

Longarm was busy trimming, warming, and lighting a slim, dark cheroot when there was a soft tap at the door and one of the huge bouncers—Longarm was not sure which this one was, but then they seemed pretty much interchangeable—stuck his head inside. "I thought you'd want to know, ma'am. I threw that fella out like you said an' tossed his clothes after him. He might could squawk when he warms up." The big man grinned. "I made him take his money out and count it before he got dressed. Just so's he'd know we don't put up with thieving here. He admitted to me that all his money was where it should be, an' there was a couple local gents handy to witness what the man said."

"Thank you, Jason. Close the door behind you now and pass the word. I don't want to be disturbed while the marshal is here with me."

"Yes, ma'am." Jason withdrew obediently, and once again Longarm had the impression that this was a very tightly run ship indeed. Whatever else Norma Brantley lacked—beauty, social graces, stuff like that—she damn sure seemed to understand the value of discipline.

"Now, Marshal. Where were we?"

"I think we were about to discuss a dead girl," Longarm told her.

Which, interestingly enough, drew no visible reaction whatsoever.

But then maybe for someone in Norma Brantley's position, the death of a young woman was not an especially remarkable event.

Chapter 12

"That would be the one who called herself Nancy," Norma Brantley said in response to Longarm's description. "Got herself killed, you say?"

"That's right."

Brantley grunted and scratched her pendulous left tit. She didn't bother trying to hide the act. "I thought she'd gone and run off. They do that sometimes, you know. Stupid cunts. They think they're in love, so they up and run off with some randy cowboy who just wants free pussy instead of having to pay for it all the time. But the cowboys convince the girls that it's true, true love and away they go. Lasts all of several weeks sometimes." The woman shook her head.

"You say her name was Nancy?" Longarm asked.

"What I said was that she called herself Nancy. God knows what her true name was. I never heard anything but Nancy."

"You don't ask the girls what their names are?"

"What for? To begin with, I don't care. And even if I did, they wouldn't tell me the truth. God, mister, don't you ever think a whore is telling you the truth. They're

58

stupid and they're venal and they lie like hell. If one of these girls tells you it's daytime, you'd best light a lamp before you step outside."

"Fond of them, aren't you?"

"Is a pig farmer fond of his sows?" Brantley said. "About that same amount, I'd say." She swiveled her chair around and fetched a goblet and decanter of something, a wine or liqueur most likely. She poured a generous measure for herself, but did not bother offering Longarm any after his earlier refusal.

"Do you know where the girl was from?" he asked.

"I know as much about that as I do her name."

"Or how old she was?"

"You saw her, and your guess would be as good as mine," Brantley countered.

"When I saw her she'd been beaten to death and was frozen solid."

"All right. Call it . . . fifteen. I've heard her tell the rubes as old as twenty-one and as young as thirteen. She could pass for either of those. What she told them all depended on what she thought they wanted to hear. An old fart with bad breath and a wheeze, he'd likely want a girl as young as he could get, so Nancy'd say she was thirteen, fourteen, something on that order. A cowboy drunk enough to think he was falling in love, she might be eighteen or twenty depending on how old he looked. The idea with that kind is for the cunt to claim she's just a year or so younger than her mark for the night. You know?"

"It's a real romantic business you're in," Longarm observed.

"Sure. So is packing salt pork into barrels. If you like your work, that is."

"You like your work, Miz Brantley?"

The woman ignored the question and took a deep swig of her tawny tipple.

"You say you'd guess she was fifteen?" Longarm asked, returning to something that at least had a prayer of being productive. Trading verbal blows with Norma Brantley surely would not be.

"It's only a guess, but yeah. About that."

"Any idea how I might find out who she was and where she came from?"

"Not really."

"Did she have any friends? Among the other girls, I mean."

Brantley shrugged, frowned, appeared to think that over. After a moment she said, "There was another girl here. That one called herself Dawn. Her and that Nancy girl used to jabber at each other and laugh and carry on together when there was no business to take care of."

"Could I talk with Dawn?" Longarm asked.

"Feel free. If you can find her."

"Did she run off with Nancy?" It occurred to Longarm that they hadn't bothered to conduct anything like a real search in the vicinity of the Travis cabin. Shit, there could be another dead girl lying about somewhere. Under the snow or tucked away in the woodpile, wherever.

"No, Dawn quit me yesterday. Little bitch. Good riddance in one way. She wasn't much account. But this is a bad time to be short-handed, what with the weather keeping everyone inside and horny."

"When was the last time you saw Nancy?"

"That would've been, I don't know . . . no, now wait a minute, yes, I do. It was Sunday. Sunday morning. We're always closed until sundown on Sundays, and the girls have the whole day off. Well, until sundown, that is. Nancy went out last Sunday morning."

"By herself?"

"As far as I know, yes."

"Could she have been on her way to church?"

That drew a snort of laughter so sudden it caught Brantley by surprise, and she let loose a small spray of wine or whatever through her nose. "Jesus, Marshal. You should know better than that."

"She wasn't going to church, I take it."

"Mister, a place like this one is popular as hell on Saturday nights. We cater to the best element. Or anybody else with cash to lay down. But come Sunday morning, the good people of Kittstown, hell, butter wouldn't melt in their mouths. Not any of them. Half, no make that three quarters of the men in town are apt to be here on any given Saturday night, including the married ones and the upright ones and the extra virtuous ones. Saturday nights they'll stick their tools into anything warm and damp that'll hold still long enough. But let one of my girls walk into their church on a Sunday morning, and she'll be lucky if they don't stone her half to death."

"You aren't suggesting . . . ?"

Brantley waved her hand in dismissal of the idea. "God, no. Whores are all stupid, but I can't think of one stupid enough to head for church of a Sunday morning. No, mister, Nancy wouldn't have done that. And no, I'm not suggesting the preacher and the elders got together to kill off a harlot." She laughed again, this time without spraying herself. "If they were going to do that, believe me, mister, they'd start with me, not with a pretty little thing like Nancy. I offend them a hell of a lot more than Nancy ever could."

"It was a thought."

"Lousy one, but yes, I suppose it was a thought."

"Let's see, you last saw Nancy on Sunday. This is,

61

what, Thursday? So she's been dead four days. I don't suppose you remember what the weather was last Sunday?"

"Look, I'm no damn almanac. And how would I know what the fucking weather was on Sunday. I never go outside hardly. I damn sure don't have reason to go out on Sundays. Now, are you about done bothering me? I have work to do here, and you aren't helping to get it done."

"One more thing."

"Make it quick."

"I assume Nancy left some personal possessions behind. What do you intend to do with those?"

"Throw the shit out, whatever of it hasn't been stolen by the other sweet young things I got here."

"I'd like to have it," Longarm said.

"You got a war . . . never mind. I don't give a shit really. I'll have Jason find it for you."

"Look, there's someplace else I need to go when I leave here, and I'd just as soon not have to lug a bunch of stuff along with me. Could you have your man drop Nancy's things off at the Jennison Arms for me?"

"You ask a lot, mister."

"I'm done asking now."

She sniffed and finished off her drink. A few seconds later she put a fist against her mouth and belched, then said, "All right. I'll have him bring the stuff to you the next time I think about it."

"I could come back tomorrow morning and—"

"All right, goddammit. This afternoon. I'll have Jason bring Nancy's crap to you this afternoon."

"Thank you, ma'am. You've been a big help."

"Well, for God's sake don't let anybody else hear you say that. My reputation is bad enough without that blemish being piled on top."

Longarm chuckled and stood. Norma Brantley was a real piece of work. "Thanks. And . . . with any kind of luck we won't meet again."

"There is that to hope for, isn't there. Go on now. You can find your own way out."

And so he could.

Chapter 13

It hadn't gotten any warmer since morning. Nor any less windy either. Longarm ducked his head to avoid the full impact of the blowing snow and trudged back along the gray, barren whips of winter-naked crack-willow until he came to the Travis cabin.

It was stupid of him to have come back, of course. This was *not* his case to worry about. Ira Parminter had made that clear enough. As a federal peace officer, Deputy Marshal Custis Long had no jurisdiction here. None.

Hell, he didn't know why he'd come back to the cabin.

All right, so he did know why. Damn it.

It was that tear frozen on the dead girl's cheek. That and her age. She'd been a kid still. Practically. Never mind what she'd been doing for a living lately. Fact was, she was just a kid. And now she was dead. And there was something about that sight of that tear frozen on her pale, no-longer-soft, and unblemished cheek that reached inside Longarm and churned his gut.

Whoever did such a thing to the girl shouldn't be allowed to walk away from it unscathed.

Never mind that Longarm had no jurisdiction. The hell with that. He would find some handle to grab hold of when the time came to sort that out. He was sure he could. He would think of something.

In the meantime, well, he wanted to take another look. That was all. Just a look. It wouldn't violate any questions of jurisdiction for him to look around. Why, the town's own mayor had invited him to look, hadn't he? Damn right, he had.

Longarm saw the dark bulk of the Travis cabin ghostly and dim through the screen of blowing snow and turned toward it.

He was nearly to the door before he realized that something seemed wrong.

For a second or two he couldn't figure out what. The place looked very much like it had the first time he arrived here, earlier in the company of the mayor.

The scene was very much the same, the door with its broken lock standing wide open and a glow of lamplight dimly visible indoors.

Except Longarm thought that Parminter had blown the lamp out before they'd left. He couldn't swear to that, but he thought it was so.

More to the point, though, was that door standing open to the storm.

Sure, the door was open this morning when Longarm and the mayor first arrived.

But it was shut when they left. Longarm knew that for a fact, for he had been the one to close it.

Had the killer come back to make sure there were no clues to his identity left behind?

Longarm tugged the glove off his left hand and reached inside his coat, drawing the big Colt from its cross-draw holster as he eased up alongside the doorway.

There was too much wind noise for him to hear anything inside. The good side to that was that no one indoors was likely to hear him over the howl of that wind either.

Longarm held his revolver poised shoulder-high and aimed in the general direction of the sky. He took a breath, braced himself in readiness, and sprang through the doorway in a rush.

Two men. No, three. Bulky. Gathered close beside the bed. They were looking down at the body, and at first remained unaware of Longarm's presence. Then one of them looked in his direction and let out a shriek of terror. He was peering straight down the sights—the wrong way—of Longarm's .44.

He screamed. His two friends turned. They screamed too.

Longarm was so startled himself that he jerked his hand sharply upward lest by some tragic error he loose off a round by accident and kill somebody.

Kids. They were a bunch of damn kids. Not much older than the boys who'd found the body to begin with. These boys were thirteen, fourteen, somewhere around there.

Enough older, anyway, to have a fascination with the sight of a naked female, never mind that she was dead and frozen.

For that was damn sure what they'd been doing. Obviously they'd heard about the naked girl from the younger kids and decided to enjoy the sight for themselves. When Longarm walked in on them, they'd been standing there holding the lamp over her and staring at the girl's body. The blanket Longarm had so carefully drawn up to cover her was pulled aside now so that these pimple-faced little pud-whackers could get an eyeful. Of a girl who couldn't possibly object to their examination.

"You little sons of bitches!" Longarm barked.

That was a mistake. He knew it almost before the sounds passed his lips.

The little bastards broke out of their rigid poses and headed for the door, taking flight as suddenly as a covey of quail breaking cover and scrambling to get by Longarm.

He wanted to talk to them. At least take down their names so as to scare the shit out of them as a lesson in manners.

He didn't have a chance. The Colt was in his right hand and they were rushing by on that side. He made a swipe at one with his left, but the kid ducked and slithered past slick as snake snot.

Even then, Longarm probably could have caught at least one of them—all right, might've had a *chance* to grab one of them—except for a rising blossom of yellow flame that he glimpsed out of the corner of his eye.

The idiot kid who'd been holding the lantern hadn't tried to take it with him when he ran. He'd just dropped the thing where he stood.

And the lantern, its globe already broken, had promptly ignited the corner of the blanket that the boys had pulled off the girl's body.

If Longarm took time to run down the boys, dammit, the cabin, body, evidence, and everything else would be a bonfire long before he could hope to get back.

With that in mind, he really didn't have much to choose from. He turned his back on the boys and hustled over to grab the burning blanket.

He set the lantern—damn thing was still burning, even after all the abuse it had taken of late—on Travis's table and carried the blanket to the door.

It didn't take much to extinguish the fire there. A little

snow did the trick. But by then, of course, there was no sign of the three boys. Little shits. Longarm hoped they hadn't taken any souvenirs with them. Like, for instance, the calling card of whoever it was who'd killed the girl known as Nancy.

Longarm cussed and grumbled some, but there really wasn't anything to be gained by that. After a few moments he shut his mouth and then the door, in that order, and went on about the business that had brought him back out there.

He hadn't thought to look for the girl's clothes before, or to go through them or her handbag, if she'd been carrying one that last day she spent on earth . . . if she'd been carrying one and if he could find it now, that is.

Not that he was conducting an investigation here or anything.

He was not.

After all, he had no jurisdiction here and so, of course, he wasn't actually looking into the case.

He just, well, wanted to be prepared. In case Mayor Parminter should happen to ask for Longarm's advice again some time in the future.

Surely there couldn't be anything wrong with that.

Longarm adjusted the wick of the much-abused lantern, then set about conducting a slow and thorough search through the Travis cabin.

Chapter 14

The technical term for what Longarm found was . . . *nada*. Nothing. Not a damn thing worth bothering with. And assorted stuff in the same useless vein.

Before he could be sure of that, though, he learned that Darby Travis had excellent taste in whiskey, which he kept hidden from casual visitors, and that the old man had enough gold dust tucked away in a cleverly hidden box to keep him in comfort for some years to come. Travis most definitely intended to return home from wherever he'd gone; no one would walk off and leave that much raw gold behind. Not even someone who'd just committed murder and panicked.

Longarm put the cabin owner's things back where he'd found them, and concentrated on the items that he was sure belonged to the girl. Those were few enough.

Her dress was plain, cheap, and much patched. Her coat was threadbare and as plain as the dress. Her shoes, on the other hand, were almost new. He suspected she must have treated herself, perhaps out of her earnings at Norma Brantley's house of happiness. Those, however, were the only things he found that he could be sure would have belonged to the girl.

If Nancy had carried a handbag with her on the Sunday past, Longarm could not find it now. Which did not prove anything. If the party or parties who killed her went in for robbery too, either as the initial reason for jumping her or possibly as an afterthought once she was dead, they very likely could have taken the handbag with them. In that case it should now be in a trash heap somewhere in or near Kittstown, or under a snowdrift, where it was likely to lie undetected until the next thaw.

As for evidence, though . . . *nada*, nothing worth a damn.

Longarm sighed and took a final look around the cabin. Nancy's body had long since been decently covered again after its violation—that, at least, was the way Longarm thought of it—by the local boys.

Hoping to repair the lock enough to avoid a repeat of that visit, he took a few minutes to examine the hasp on the cabin door, and discovered that it was doubly busted. Not only was the padlock broken, the screws holding the iron hasp had been jimmied out of the rotting wood and then pressed finger-tight back in place.

Longarm found that to be at least mildly interesting. Not that he'd ever had any idea that Darby Travis was a suspect in the killing, but this pretty much proved it. After all, Darby Travis had a key and did not need to bust up his own property.

The youngsters who reported the body to the mayor admitted to breaking the padlock.

So it must have been Nancy's killer who pried the hasp loose.

Damn it anyway, Longarm thought. Why couldn't the son of a bitch have left something, forgotten something, given some sort of indication of who or what he was?

There was nothing.

Longarm closed the door and wedged a scrap of wood

under it to keep it from being blown open by the swirling winds, then arranged the jimmied hasp and broken lock so that from a distance they would give the appearance, false though it was, of being intact.

Maybe that would be enough to keep any more gawkers from sneaking in.

And tomorrow, if he could, or anyway as soon as the storm permitted, Longarm figured to have whoever it was in Kittstown who provided mortuary services pick the girl's body up and see that it was properly attended.

The thought of Nancy, so young and so pretty and with that tear frozen on her cheek, lying abandoned in a frigid shack with nothing but pack rats for company . . . that bothered Longarm.

Dammit, he would see that the girl was taken care of if he had to pay for the burial out of his own pocket.

He pulled the fur cap low on his forehead, turned his coat collar high, and set out into the force of the storm once more.

He was already back in town, walking in the lee of a block of tall buildings where the wind was broken and there was a sense of relative warmth, when someone took a shot at him.

Chapter 15

It sounded like the world biggest bumblebee zipping and sizzling past his left ear. Except no bee alive could ever fly that fast. And there weren't a whole hell of a lot of bees that went out for a look-see in the middle of a Wyoming blizzard.

Besides, Longarm was kinda cheating when he recognized the sound of the bullet; he'd heard its like many a time before.

Not that he was standing there thinking all this through, though. By the time he consciously realized the importance of the sound, he was already burrowing face-first into a snowdrift piled against the north wall of the alley and already had his revolver in hand.

Drifted snow made a damn poor barrier against gunfire, so he didn't tarry.

He came rolling back onto bare, frozen earth with the Colt pointed more or less in the direction from which the shot was fired.

More or less, that is, because it was all blind guesswork. *Literally* blind guesswork. Longarm had a face full of snow that was packed thick on his eyes and in

72

his nose and had the same sharp, ozone smell as winter air.

He spat and pawed the snow off his face and blinked wildly as he rolled first one way and then the other, trying to keep the ambusher from getting any luckier with a second shot.

The sonuvabitch fired again, sending up a spray of ice chips and dirt from just to Longarm's left, but this time the gunman's target was face-on to him, and this time Longarm had vision enough to see the muzzle flash from the side of the building at the far back end of the alley.

Longarm snapped a shot off in return, swiped impatiently at the small clods and loose dusting of snow that continued to hamper his vision, then took more careful aim and blew some splinters off the wood trim at the back of the building.

There was no howl of pain and no satisfying thump of a body hitting the ground, so he had to figure he'd missed.

But he bet he'd come close enough to make the crotch of the bastard's britches wet.

He rubbed at his eyes again and, able to see clearly, rolled quickly to his right and sprang onto his feet.

There was no movement at the far end of the alley. Close and cautious inspection disclosed that the gunman, whoever the son of a bitch was, had given up, at least for the time being.

Longarm stood in the lee of the structure that had sheltered the ambusher and gave the matter some serious thought while his hands were occupied with reloading the big .44.

When he was done he had reached two conclusions. The first was that the gunman—he thought he knew who it pretty much had to be—would not likely make a second attempt on his life.

The second was that, all in all, it really wasn't such a bad thing that the asshole had tried to backshoot him. Not, that is, since he'd missed.

In fact, dammit, the incident could turn out to be a downright positive event.

With a grunt of satisfaction Longarm returned the Colt to its holster—discovering as he did so that he'd snatched the gun out so fast and so automatically that he'd torn a button off the belly of his coat while he was at it—then headed off in the direction of Kittstown's business district.

Chapter 16

"Afternoon, Mr. Mayor," Longarm said, closing the storm outside and removing his hat and gloves. The inside of the mercantile was oppressively hot. Which seemed mighty comfortable after spending so much time out in the blizzard that continued its efforts to bury southern Wyoming.

"Deputy," Parminter said by way of greeting.

"You open for business, Mr. Mayor? I need a button to go on this here coat."

"I'm sure I can find something for you." Parminter fetched a wooden box down from a shelf and began rummaging through it. Longarm stepped closer, and saw that it was a box of mismatched buttons ranging from tiny collar buttons to tough shoe buttons and up as large as some huge, decorative buttons. The materials used were almost everything: horn, bone, antler, tortoise shell, assorted metals, even a few gleaming bits of abalone.

"I think this one might match," Parminter suggested.

"Close enough." Longarm dropped the button into his pocket. "Thanks. How much do I owe you?"

"No charge. Glad to help. Uh, I've been hearing that

you are looking into that girl's death. Is that true, Marshal?''

"Into the murder, you mean?"

"Murder, accident, whatever."

"I've asked a few questions, that's all."

"You know, of course, that you have no jurisdiction here," the mayor reminded him. "Not unless I specifically ask for your help."

"Is there something about this that you wanta hide, Mr. Mayor?"

"Of course not. I just don't want the community stirred up over nothing."

"Nothing, sir? She was a girl. A human person with feelings just the same as yours or mine."

"She was a whore."

"Yes, sir. A living, breathing, female human whore. And she didn't deserve to die just because of what she was doing for a living."

"I'm not trying to argue that point with you, Deputy. I just don't want a lot of trouble caused over this." Parminter took in a deep breath, held it a moment, and slowly let it out. "Can I be honest with you, Deputy?"

"I kinda wish you would, Mr. Mayor."

"Kittstown is undergoing a . . . what you might call a crisis right now."

"How's that, sir?"

"As you may already know, the powers that be in the Territory of Wyoming have chosen to extend a limited voting franchise to, well, to women. Women are allowed to register and to vote in certain local elections. And there is talk that if Wyoming is admitted to statehood, women will be allowed to vote in all elections at the state level and below. Not in matters of national importance, of course. But already they are allowed to take a voice, by way of the actual ballot box, that is, in municipal affairs.

"My personal opinion is that this is a great mistake. Women haven't the judgment nor the education nor, frankly, the critical abilities needed to arrive at decisions like this."

Longarm knew better than to put an oar into that water. Neither for the mayor's view nor against it, because this was the sort of thing that could lead to more talk later in circumstances that an unwise speaker might not even know about. It was one of those questions about which everyone's mind seemed downright solidly made up, and no one was much interested in having his opinions changed. Especially by anything as inconsequential as mere fact. There was no way you could fight emotion with logic, and Longarm wasn't fixing to try. "Yes, sir," was all Longarm said. He was much more interested in listening right now than in talking anyway.

"There are some women in Kittstown, you see, who are rather loudly demanding that we . . . the city council, that is . . . um, well, pass new laws to, as they put it, clean up the community. No prostitution at all, you see. No gambling. There are even some rabble-rousers who say we should prohibit the sale or consumption of alcoholic beverages within the town limits. Can you imagine that?"

"And you're afraid—"

"I am very much afraid that any public commotion that draws attention to the presence of open prostitution in this community, especially in such an unsavory way as murder, well, I'm afraid it could cause the sort of backlash that would do harm to a great many people in Kittstown."

"Have to shut Norma Brantley down, maybe the Old Heidelberg too, and all the other saloons as well?"

"It could get that bad, yes."

"I hope for your sake and for that of all the other menfolk in town, sir, that it won't have to come to that. But the truth is, sir, that one of the things I came by to tell you is that I've taken jurisdiction in the murder of the girl known as Nancy."

"Nancy. Yes, I remember her now. God, she was a pretty little thing. Sweet too. She didn't know many tricks in bed, but she was a nice girl. I . . . I have to confess that I was with her once myself. I'm ashamed to admit that I wasn't sure when I saw her this morning. She looked . . . smaller in death. And so pale. I should have remembered better than that, shouldn't I?" Parminter had been fumbling with his hands, eyes downcast. Now he looked up, his eyes becoming wide with anxiety. "You say you have assumed jurisdiction, Marshal? You can't do that. Not without my specific invitation. We talked about this before. Don't you remember?"

"That was accurate then, Mr. Mayor. Things've changed since."

"Changed? I don't understand."

"A little while ago your murderer took a shot at me. It was in an alley a couple blocks over."

"I'm glad you survived, of course, and shocked to think that anyone here would do a thing like that. But . . . how does that change things to give you jurisdiction in a purely local matter, Deputy?"

"Assault on a federal officer, Mr. Mayor, is a federal crime. Soon as that jehu pulled the trigger, he opened the door for me to put my nose into this thing just as far and just as deep as I can ram it."

"I don't—"

"I've already been over to the telegraph office, sir. I sent a message to my boss, Marshal Vail, back in Denver

78

telling him that I'm assuming jurisdiction over the objection of local authority. Naturally you're welcome to contact him your own self to confirm what I say or to protest what I did. Whatever you think best, sir.''

It would hold up, though. Longarm knew damned good and well that not only would Billy Vail back him in this, so would the Justice Department.

Of course, that would be assuming Longarm never mentioned what he really believed had happened in that alley back there.

That gunshot had been a gift. Because surely the truth was that it was hot-tempered and stupid George who had tried to pot a marshal for dinner. Without fully knowing what it was he was doing.

Hell, there wasn't anyone else around Kittstown who could possibly have any sort of hard-on for Longarm.

Nancy's murderer had nothing to fear from him because, as a federal officer, Longarm hadn't been after him. For the murderer to shoot at Longarm and open this exact same door would have been an example of stupidity in the extreme.

But dumb and feisty George, he was another matter entirely.

Longarm had thought about George at some length and realized a couple things. And far and away the most important of those was that George seemed to be one of the few people in Kittstown who didn't know who Longarm was. That is, didn't know that Longarm was a deputy United States marshal.

Longarm had told that to practically everybody else he came in contact with, those few who hadn't already known and greeted him with the information themselves.

But as he thought back over the times he'd encountered George, each of them hostile to one degree or another, he realized that neither he nor anybody else had ever mentioned to the idiot that the tall guy with the big Colt happened to be a peace officer.

So back in that alley George was likely venting his spleen some. And just as likely, he didn't really want to shoot anyone, Longarm concluded after thinking the thing through.

No, the most likely way to put this on the string was that George and his little pocket gun were just wanting to make some loud noises so that old George could feel like the he-man he really wasn't. For George, it was just a way to get back some self-respect. Not that he deserved any, but that wasn't the question here.

As for the real murderer, Longarm suspected the very *last* thing he wanted was to give Longarm an excuse to come in on the case. Unlike George, the real murderer probably would have taken any manner of abuse rather than allow that to happen.

Well, now it had gone and happened anyway.

Officially, that is.

There was no way Longarm was going to tell Ira Parminter, Billy Vail, or anyone else about this, of course.

Officially, the only logical explanation for the shooting was as a response to his probing out at the Travis cabin.

And it could damn well stay that way, no matter what the mayor of Kittstown might prefer.

"Sorry, Mr. Mayor. I, uh, I've written out Marshal Vail's address here, and already left word with the telegraph operator that you may need him shortly. He was fixing to close up and go home early, but I told him you might want him first. If you decide not to get a wire off to the marshal, sir, you might wanta tell that telegrapher so he can lock up."

"I don't know what to say," Parminter mumbled.

"Nothing needs to be said now, sir."

"This could be a disaster for Kittstown."

"Not if the menfolk get together and vote the women down, sir."

"But if they do that . . ."

Longarm shrugged. "I've always believed a man should stand up and be seen, whether others agree with him or not. But then that's only my opinion, sir, and I don't have to live here. You and the men of Kittstown will have to work out your votes and your problems for your own selves, I expect. Now if you'll excuse me, sir . . ."

Longarm pulled his hat and gloves back on and headed for the door. He paused there for a moment. "Thank you for the button, sir. Good-bye now."

Chapter 17

Stupid, miserable, sonuvabitching, stinking, damned
SNOW! Longarm was tired of it. Days and days it'd
been blowing now and no end in sight. He was tired of
it, dammit. He'd had enough of it. He . . . he stopped
practically in mid-stride, unmindful of the cold wind that
was stinging his eyes and making his nose drool cold
snot into his mustache.

He grinned and snapped his fingers.

Nancy's friend Dawn. He knew where she was. Or
anyway, where she pretty much had to be right now.

Norma Brantley had gone and told him where to find
her. It was just that neither she nor Longarm had noticed
it at the time.

Longarm turned back the way he'd just come and an-
gled across the street. He tried to whistle a light, gay
tune. Unfortunately, his lips were so cold he couldn't
get them to shape the notes he wanted, and he ended up
repeating the same weak tone over and over again.

"Marshal." The woman greeted him with a pleasant
enough nod.

"Ma'am." He made a small bow and swept the fur hat off. And hoped the gesture was not ruined by icicles of frozen snot or anything of such an unsightly nature.

"Is there something I can do for you?" she asked.

"If you don't mind, Mrs. Forsyth."

The boss lady of the Old Heidelberg motioned with an upraised finger, and seconds later there was a glass of most excellent rye whiskey on the table in front of Longarm. He tasted it, smiled, and thanked her.

"My pleasure," she said. "Now, sir . . . what is it that you require?"

"I believe you took on a new employee yesterday," he said. "Calls herself Dawn, I think. Or anyhow, that's the name she used over at, uh, the other place where she used to work."

"You have excellent sources of information, Marshal."

"No better than yours, I think." The truth, of course, was simple enough. Yesterday the girl had quit Norma Brantley. And according to Brantley, Kittstown would not likely welcome one of Brantley's girls in any other, more innocent capacity. If she intended to stay here it would have to be as a whore. And did she intend to stay here? Since it was yesterday when she quit, her intentions really didn't matter; in the continuing snowstorm she had no choice but to stay. Hence there was only one other place where she could be, and that was here at the Old Heidelberg.

"Dawn will continue to use that name here." Amanda Forsyth shrugged. "So many of the gents already know her by that name, don't you see."

"Sure. No sense in confusing anyone."

"Exactly."

"I'd like to have a few minutes of conversation with this Dawn girl."

"Of course, Marshal. She is . . . never mind, I need to pass by that way anyway. I'll show you where to find her."

Longarm polished off the rye—it was much too good to waste—and followed Mrs. Forsyth upstairs.

"This way, Marshal." The lady—she was an almighty fine figure of a woman—tapped lightly on a door that had no numbers or other distinguishing marks on it. "Dawn? Open up, dear."

The girl who answered her employer's summons was not much older than Nancy had been. Dawn, or whatever her true name was, was tall and slender, with black hair drawn back in a severe bun. With the bun and a pair of silver-framed spectacles, she had something of a school-mistress look about her. Almost prim. Almost proper. Almost. The effect was somewhat hampered by the threadbare kimono that she held gathered in one hand at her waist, her shoulders, legs, and swelling breasts bare for all the world to see. "Yes, ma'am?"

"This gentleman is a United States deputy marshal, Dawn. He wants to talk to you. I expect you to answer whatever questions he may have."

"Yes, ma'am."

"Also, Dawn, I promised him the use of one of my girls. Do anything else he asks you to also. At no charge to him, of course."

"Yes, ma'am."

"Thank you, Dawn." She turned to Longarm. "If you need me for anything, Marshal, I will be in my office. It is the last door at the end of the corridor."

"Thanks."

Amanda Forsyth bobbed her head in farewell and continued at what Longarm thought a rather regal gait off in the direction of the office.

84

He watched the lady go, then turned back to the girl who called herself Dawn.

While his attention was elsewhere she had shed the kimono, and was now standing naked before him.

Chapter 18

"Pretty," he said, allowing his gaze to run up and down the length of the naked girl.

"Thanks, but would you mind shutting the damn door."

"Oh, yeah. Sorry." He winked at her and stepped inside, closing the door behind him.

"Now, mister . . ."

Longarm took out a cheroot, nipped the twist off it with his teeth, and took his time about getting it lighted.

"Do you just wanta look, mister, or do you wanta screw?"

"Neither one of those," he told her, giving the coal and budding ash a critical inspection. "I think this one side of my smokes got a little damp somehow," he mused aloud.

"Well, mister, I'm just real awful sorry about that. You know?"

"Thanks for the sympathy, I'm sure."

"You don't wanta look and you don't wanta screw. So just what the hell *do* you want me to do anyhow?"

"Just like the lady said, Dawn. I want to talk to you."

"That's all? Just talk?"

"Just talk," he affirmed.

"If you say so. You want me to cover up?"

He grinned at her. "Not particularly. The view is just fine from here."

Dawn laughed, shrugged, and plopped herself down on the side of the bed, still quite fetchingly naked. He noticed now that she had a small, strawberry birthmark—or was it a tattoo; surely not—just at the top edge of her pubic hair, which was thick and dark and curly. Nice-looking tits. Flat belly. Small waist. When seen like this, there was not much chance that she would be mistaken for a schoolmarm. On the other hand . . . "Do you know what you look like?" he asked.

"Hell, yes, honey. And d'you know what? I used to be one. I taught the primary grades at . . . well, never mind where it was. But it's true. I taught the little bastards . . . little darlings, that is"—she made a face, then laughed at herself—"for almost three years before I discovered there were easier ways to make a living."

"Easier?"

"That's the idea anyhow."

"And is it easier?"

Dawn shrugged again. "When a girl is dumb enough to get herself knocked up by the president of the school board, she all of a sudden finds out that teaching can get real difficult. But shit, that isn't what you wanted to talk about, I'm sure."

"No, young lady, what I want is to learn about your friend Nancy."

"She's dead, isn't she?"

Longarm nodded.

"Everybody in the bar is talking about it. They said some little boys found her all frozen and stiff. They said she was beat up so bad she died from it. They said she was all black and blue and ugly. Is that true, mister?"

"Yes, it is. I'm sorry."

Dawn's eyes filled, but she bit down hard on her lower lip and kept the tears from flowing. "She was a good kid."

"Tell me about her. Please."

"How come, mister? She wasn't nothing but a whore. Nobody gives a damn when a whore gets beat to death."

"Me," Longarm said. "I give a damn. I intend to find whoever it was that killed her."

"Something else I heard tell, mister, is that you're a federal man and can't do or say nothing about how the law is handled here."

Longarm smiled. "I hope others believe that same thing, Dawn. I hope the truth comes as a real nasty surprise for somebody."

"You really want to find who it was that killed her?"

"I damn sure do. I want to find out who killed her, and I want to find her family too so they can be informed and hopefully get that girl's body back. She should be buried with her own."

"If you really and truly mean that, then listen, mister. Anything I can do to help you, I mean anything at all, you just ask for it and I'll jump to lend you a hand. Nancy, she was about the best friend I've had since . . . well, since a real long time ago. I liked her a lot, and I'd be a pretty poor friend if I stood back now and didn't help when I could. So you just ask, mister. Anything at all. If I can't stand to tell you the truth, at least I won't tell you no lies. Is that all right?"

"That sounds fair to me, Dawn."

"Sit down, mister, and let's you and me talk." She patted the slightly soiled sheet beside her pale, pretty rump.

Longarm accepted the invitation.

Chapter 19

"Her name really was Nancy," the girl who called herself Dawn said. "Isn't that about the craziest thing you ever heard? She was using her real name. I mean, Nancy was honestly that dumb when it came to some things. I guess I shouldn't say 'dumb,' should I? Speak ill of the dead and all that stuff?"

"Naive maybe?" Longarm suggested.

Dawn smiled. "That sounds a lot nicer, doesn't it."

"Go on, please. What was the rest of her name?"

"I don't know."

Longarm raised an eyebrow.

"No, don't look at me like that, mister. I'm telling you the truth. Nancy was . . . what was that word you used? . . . she was real naive some ways. But she was learning." Dawn gave him a wan little half smile. "A girl learns real quick when she goes into the life. You know?"

"Yeah, I can imagine," he said. Although in truth he probably could not. Not really. Probably no male ever really could.

"Well, Nancy, she was learning. She talked about her

family a lot. She missed them. But she never told me what their family name was. A couple times she mentioned them being Smith or Jones. But the way she said it made it clear that she wasn't telling me the truth. And she wanted me to know that that wasn't really her name. It was like she wanted to protect them from even being mentioned under the roof of a whorehouse.''

"Was she ashamed of what she did?'' Longarm asked.

"Christ, what are you? Some kind of innocent lamb? Everybody is ashamed of working in a whorehouse. Except maybe some of the men. The bouncers, I mean. They like it. But that's because they get to fuck all the girls and don't have to pay for it. They think that's something to brag about to all the other guys, I guess.''

"But the girls?''

"Mister, nobody starts out in life and thinks, gee, I'd like to grow up and be a whore. You know? You ever see any little doll-babies dressed in short skirts or kimonos, stuff for little girls to play with and imagine themselves growing up to wear powder a pound at a time or lie around being like a public toilet for drunks to squirt off into? You think my dream when I was a kid was to suck the cock of some horny bastard that hasn't taken a bath in six months? Mister, this business is something a girl just kinda lucks out on.'' Her short, hard yap of laughter sounded something like the bark of a seal. But it contained somewhat less humor.

"Was it that way for Nancy too?''

"Of course it was. She was dumb. Like all the rest of us. And even younger than most. I mean, I started when I was nineteen. I was grown. But poor little Nancy, she wasn't hardly past her fifteenth birthday when she was turned out.''

"Turned out?''

"That's what you call it, getting started into the life. A girl is said to've been turned out when she's turned her first full trick. Not just blow jobs, mind. Little girls whose mamas are whores can give blow jobs from the time they're five or six. That stuff doesn't count. When you're turned out is when you've gotten paid for a real fuck for the first time. Of course, a girl going into the business will have lost her cherry a long time before that. Usually to an uncle or a traveling salesman or some such sharpie. And then, of course, whoever the boss is and the bouncers, they'll always use a girl for a while to sort of get her started under saddle." Dawn laughed. "That's the way the cowboys talk about it. Started under saddle. It kind of fits, don't you think?"

Longarm didn't answer. He pretended to be busy with his cheroot.

"Where were we? Oh, yeah . . . Nancy. She was just past turning fifteen when she started. That was at a house in Cheyenne."

"Cheyenne. Is that where she's from?"

"No, I'm sure she wasn't. She said something about . . . what the hell was the name of that town anyway? She talked about it sometimes. It was way east of Cheyenne. In Nebraska somewhere, I think. Freedom? Freeman? Free-something."

"Fremont?" Longarm asked.

"That sounds right. Sure. Fremont."

Fremont, Nebraska. Longarm knew the place. Not well, but he'd been there before. Sort of the way he'd known Kittstown before. Not well. But enough. So the child was Nancy from Fremont.

"Do you know why she became, uh . . ."

"A whore? Look, mister, it's okay for you to say it. I mean, it isn't like it's something I've never heard before, and it isn't an insult unless you say it nasty-like. I mean, Nancy was a whore. I'm a whore. It's the truth. Okay?''

"Sure." He drew on the cheroot and waited for Dawn to go on.

"As for why Nancy took to the life, that's pretty simple. It's the same for most of us. She had to make a living somehow, and this seemed a good way. Easy. Good money." Dawn made a face and laughed a little bit. Perhaps, Longarm thought, the money wasn't all that good, no matter what a body might expect to the contrary.

"I mean," Dawn said, "it wasn't like she had a reputation to protect or anything like that. She was already a slut as far as her folks was concerned."

"How's that?" Longarm asked.

Dawn shrugged. "The usual shit. She was making it in the hayloft with some fella. In her case it was the preacher. One of those hellfire-and-damnation types that gets everybody all worked up and then needs some way to let down afterward. Well, with this one, according to what Nancy said, she was the one chosen to help him out with his good work. Help him out of his difficulty and into her drawers, plain and simple. Except, of course, she didn't know a dick from a doorknob. She just knew that this preacher wouldn't never ever lie to her and if he said something was all right, then of course it was all right. And he told her this was her duty, her path to salvation." Dawn snorted. "The bastard put her on the path, all right, but not to salvation. Then when Nancy missed her period and her mother noticed that she wasn't asking for rags to use at that time of month, her mother got to questioning her and it came out. The preacher denied the whole thing and prayed over her and accused her of fucking some neighbor boy, which she swore she never did, and her folks called her a harlot and a liar and all the usual shit. And so she sneaked out in the middle of the night and talked her way onto a westbound train. One of the brakemen let her ride in the caboose. Poor innocent Nancy. She didn't know she'd have to pay the rent in exchange.''

''Pardon me?''

''Pay the rent,'' Dawn explained. ''She had to put out for the brakeman and his buddies in the caboose. All of them. It wasn't the sort of thing she'd had in mind, see, but then she didn't have any choice about it once they got started. And of course it didn't kill her. It wasn't much different with those guys than it'd been with the preacher. So when they put her off the train in Cheyenne, well, she knew by then she was damaged goods, as the saying goes, and no point pretending to be Miss Goody-Goody. She had nothing and she had nobody, but she knew how to spread her legs. And she was pretty. She really was, you know. So pretty. And so sweet.'' Dawn sighed. ''So that's how she got into the life. A real ordinary story, you know?''

''What about the baby?'' Longarm asked. ''Where is the baby?''

Dawn chuckled, but there was no hint of mirth in the sound. ''That's a real pisser, mister. Turns out she wasn't knocked up after all. It was just a false alarm. Isn't that just about the funniest damn thing you ever did hear?''

''Yeah,'' he said in a dry, sad voice. ''Damn well hilarious.''

Chapter 20

Longarm walked to the window and peered unfocused into an unseen distance. He could not actually have looked out through the glass had he wanted to. It was frosted over a quarter-inch thick or more, and he could feel the chill seeping through his clothes to find vulnerable flesh when he stood near the frozen glass. He stood there for several minutes, smoking, thinking about the dead girl-child Nancy. Then he tossed the butt of his cheroot into a rusting can that served as a makeshift spittoon and went back to sit again on the side of the bed next to Dawn.

Who, he could not help but notice, had not made any attempt to cover herself. She was still naked. And getting prettier as the minutes passed.

"Tell me about last Sunday morning," he said.

Dawn turned her face away and seemed to collect her thoughts. Finally she spoke. "I guess that's why I feel so extra bad about what happened to Nancy," she said.

"How's that?"

"Saturday nights are always real busy, but Nancy, she never was one to sleep in late. She had the habit of rising early no matter what. Me, I'll sleep till way past noon if I can get away with it." She tried for a small smile and almost managed one. "That's one of the advantages of my line of work, if you see what I mean."

"Sure."

"Last Sunday, though, I was awake early for some reason. I wasn't sick or nothing like that. Just awake. Nancy came by, oh, about ten o'clock I think it was. She didn't knock. Prob'ly she didn't want to wake me if I was still asleep. She just opened the door and peeped in. I saw her and said good morning, and she slipped inside and sat on the edge of the bed. Right there where you are now, 'cept in the other place instead of here. She sat right down and reached over and took my hand. Her hand was cold, I remember. I suppose she'd been out to the backhouse already, then come back inside to get ready to go out. Anyway, her hand was cold. I remember that so plain. I can as good as still feel it. You know?"

He nodded, encouraging Dawn to continue but not wanting to interrupt the flow of her thoughts.

"She held my hand in both of hers and said, 'Dawn, why don't you come out with me. It's such a beautiful morning. Come walk with me.' Nancy loved to get up, sometimes real early, and go walking. Not to any place in particular. She just liked to walk in the mornings. She said the air was clean and sweet then and the walking made her feel good. She asked me to come along any number of times, and I always thought that one of these days I would do it. But the way it turns out, I never did and I never will.

"But I wanted to. Really I did. But I'd worked awful hard the night before and the bed felt so soft and warm and it was cold outside. Had been for a couple weeks already. There wasn't no snow yet. Not but a few little flurries every now and then, but there wasn't no snow

95

sticking on the ground yet. That was still to come.

"And anyway, Nancy wanted me to come out with her and in a way I wanted to, but in the end I decided to stay under the covers and let Nancy go on alone." Dawn gave Longarm a haunted, stricken look. "If I'd got my ass out of bed that morning and gone with her . . ."

"If you'd done that," Longarm said, "then more than likely you both would be dead today. It wouldn't have done Nancy the least bit of good." Not that he believed that. The truth was that if there had been two girls strolling together, then today they almost certainly would both be alive. But that was not what Dawn needed to hear right now.

"Do you remember what she was wearing?" he asked.

"Every stitch," Dawn said. And she proceeded to describe to perfection the women's clothes Longarm had found at the Travis cabin.

"Was she carrying a handbag that day, can you recall?" he asked next.

Again Dawn gave the question thought before she answered. "I'm sure she was. I think . . . yes, she put it down beside her. On the far side of her. I remember seeing the handle of it visible beside her thigh."

"The handle. Could you describe the bag for me?" There was no handbag at the cabin. Longarm was certain of that.

"It's an old bag. Nancy never said, but I think maybe it was her mama's bag or somebody special to her like that. She was real fond of it. I remember a couple weeks ago we were shopping. We're allowed to shop on Wednesday afternoons, you see. The decent women don't come into the shops on Wednesdays between three and five. They stay home cooking and getting ready for prayer meetings or quilting bees or whatever, and us whores are allowed to conduct our business then when we won't contaminate any of the fine ladies or be seen by them. Nancy and me were shopping, and she bought herself some new shoes. Her old ones were falling to pieces. She'd tried sewing them with twine I don't know how many times, but they'd gotten too bad even for her to put up with. Anyhow, she bought herself some new shoes—God, Nancy was so tight with a penny you'd think she intended to breed them or something—and I saw this pretty little handbag that would've looked so awful nice with those shoes, and I told her she ought to get that too, but she wouldn't. She said her old bag had done for many and many a year, and she expected it would keep right on doing. And of course Nancy herself wasn't old enough to've carried a handbag for years, so it pretty much had to have had sentimental value because of somebody else.''

"That sounds right," Longarm agreed. "Do you remember what it looked like?"

"Of course. It had a pair of curved wicker handles and was about this big''—she indicated with her hands—''pretty good-sized really, and it was made out of a thick tapestry material, mostly black with a green and yellow and white pattern embroidered all over. The pattern was birds in the middle, surrounded by leaves and flowers.''

Longarm didn't bother to ask if Dawn was sure. He was positive that she was.

But he damn sure hadn't seen any bag of that nature at Darby Travis's place.

"Do you know if Nancy intended to meet anyone that morning?" he asked.

"Who would a whore go off to meet?"

"A customer maybe?" Longarm suggested.

97

"Not Nancy. She'd had her belly full—in more ways than one—when it came to men. She'd fuck one for pay, but she hadn't any more interest in men than she did in cows. Either one was just something you might see alongside the road."

"You're sure that—"

"Look, mister, I'm being honest with you, okay? I mean, I really want you to find whoever it was did that to Nancy. She was a sweet girl. But I can absolutely, positively guarantee you that she didn't go off to see no man that morning. And she didn't need to go anywhere if she wanted to see a woman. You know what I'm telling you? Norma, she's as bad as the men who run most houses. A girl always has to sleep with the boss free for nothing. Over across town it's Norma that the girls have to sleep with. And Nancy, she took to that real well. I mean, I suppose it isn't speaking ill of the dead if it's the simple truth, is it?"

"No, of course not."

"Well, the truth is that Nancy would fuck a man for business, but for fun she wanted to be with a woman. She asked me more than once. But that isn't what I like. You know? I mean, I've done it. I had to when I worked for Norma, just like all the other girls there. But it was something I did to get it over with and get on with other things. Nancy liked it. So if she was going to take a lover, mister, it wouldn't have been some client. It would have been one of the other girls."

"I see. Is, uh, there anything else you can think of that I should know?"

Dawn shook her head.

"If you think of anything, I'm staying at the Jennison Arms. You've already been a big help, and I thank you." He stood.

Dawn reached for his hand and tugged him closer to her.

"Yes?" Before he knew what she was up to, she had the buttons of his fly unfastened and the limp sausage of his cock warm and wet inside her mouth.

"I didn't mean . . ." But Dawn reached up to place a finger over his lips to hush him. She shook her head no. Which felt almighty good under the circumstances. And of a sudden he was no longer limp.

He hadn't, he really and truly hadn't meant for anything remotely like this to happen.

But now that it was . . .

"I can't . . ."

But that was a lie. The truth was that he damn sure could.

Chapter 21

Longarm lit another cheroot and made his way down-stairs to the bar. He was more than a little confused. After all, the girl had told him point-blank that, to her and to other girls like her, men were just a business proposition. Then she'd gone and done what she'd done. And had acted as if she enjoyed it. As if she was the one wanting it. He couldn't really understand that.

Unless she wanted something else. But if that was the case . . . what the hell was it? Not money. The boss had told her anything Longarm wanted was to be on the house, and sure enough, Dawn hadn't asked for a cent.

So what was it that she wanted from him?

He shook his head. Either he would find out eventually, in which case he could deal with it then, or perhaps he never would know. In which case it might damn well drive him crazy trying to figure it out.

Either way, though, it would keep for the time being.

"Rye again?" the barman asked.

Longarm nodded and laid a quarter on the bar. The bartender poured a pair of drinks—from the good but not quite absolutely marvelous bottle, Longarm noted—and turned away without comment.

"Hey! Longarm. Over here."

The quartet of friendly cowboys was at a table dealing cards. One of them, it took him a moment to bring the names back to mind, waved and motioned for him to join them.

"I'm in," Longarm responded. He knocked back his first drink and carried the second with him to the table. The whiskey was warm and welcome as it spread through his belly.

The young fellow who'd called out to him, Jason he was, reached around and dragged a fifth chair between his place and that of Ronnie Gordon. "Sit down, Marshal. The game is straight draw poker. Nothing wild and nothing fancy. Nickel to ante, and I happen to notice that you're light."

Longarm grinned and dug into a pocket to find whatever loose change he had on him. He pushed a nickel into the center of the table and leaned back, relaxed and quite content now with cards in one hand, a cheroot in the other, and a shot of rye nesting in his belly.

"Shit!" Longarm barked. He folded his cards and tossed them down.

"You haven't even looked at those yet."

"Huh? Oh. That ain't what I'm bitching about. Deal around me, boys. I'll be right back." Longarm stood, his legs feeling cramped after an hour or so sitting in one place. He felt a tightness at the nape of his neck and a swelling across his shoulders. Across the way, just coming inside, was that asshole George and the scrawny pal who ran with him. Longarm figured them for a pair of genuine sons of bitches.

He crossed the room in long strides and met George as the man was unbuttoning his coat.

"You," George snarled when he saw Longarm approach. "I ought to—"

He did not have time to finish the sentence, whatever it might have been.

Longarm's hand shot forward, locking onto George's neck immediately under the shelf of the man's jaw. Instead of squeezing, Longarm pushed. And lifted. He drove George back against the wall and up several inches so that he was held suspended just off the floor, dangling in place with the heels of his shoes drumming against the cold boards of the street-side wall.

"Ack . . . ish . . . awk . . ." George choked and sputtered and gagged, but could not get any words out.

"Shut your fucking mouth," Longarm snapped. "Shut up and listen close, you bag of puke." He reached inside his own coat and yanked out his wallet, snapping it open with a flick of his wrist so that he could push his badge hard against the bridge of George's nose. "You see this, little man? Do you?"

George couldn't speak, but he managed a nod.

"Assault on a federal officer is a federal crime. You mess with me, Harry, and I'll have your ass in Leavenworth Prison for the next five years. Do you understand me? Do you hear what I'm telling you?"

George nodded again.

"You, your buddy there, some piece of shit you decide to hire, any or all of you come at me, Harry, and it's you that I'll put in irons and drag off for prosecution. You got that now? Am I making myself perfectly clear?"

George nodded. He was getting better at it with practice.

"I hope so, because one more incident, anything at all, and your butt is mine. You got that?" The guy was turning purple. Longarm let him slide down the wall far enough that he was able to take his weight on his own feet. "You got that, Harry?"

"Y-yes, sir. But I didn't do anything. I swear to you, I never—"

Longarm tightened his grip on George's neck, squeezing enough with his thumb to cut off the circulation of blood to the man's head. "When I want to hear your lies I'll ask for some. Until then you keep your mouth shut. Understand me?"

George nodded. That was not only easier than speaking, it seemed safer as well with the mood Longarm was in at the moment.

"Where's your gun?" Longarm demanded.

"H . . . h . . ." Longarm relaxed his grip a little. "Hotel," George said. "In my room. Didn't . . . didn't want any trouble again. I left it in my room."

Longarm grunted and felt the man's coat pockets, then around his waistband. He did not seem to be carrying the pistol.

"You're lucky, Harry. You got your warning. Next time I'll either take you into custody or just up and shoot you. Do you hear me?"

"Next time? But I didn't—" Longarm squeezed. George shut up.

"Remember what I told you. Any more shit outa you and the best you can hope for is five years behind bars. And that's if you're lucky enough to live so long. Now get the hell out of here. I don't want to have to wonder what you're doing behind my back."

Longarm let go of the thoroughly frightened fellow. George turned and scuttled out of the saloon without so much as pausing to button his coat shut again.

George's friend gave Longarm a dirty look, but did not try to follow the thoughts with any actions. After a moment he too turned and made a quick exit.

Longarm wound up feeling growly as a bear just coming out of hibernation. He went over to the bar and helped himself to a pickled egg and some cheese off the free lunch spread, paid for a round of beers to be delivered to the table where his place was still waiting, and spent a few moments alone so that he could calm down before he got back to the game.

Bastard, Longarm thought. Miserable, backshooting little son of a flea-bitten bitch.

Still, he was pretty sure he wouldn't have to worry about George again.

After another minute or so he lit a cheroot and let the flavor of the pale smoke soothe and mollify him. Then he went back to the card game and the inevitable excited questions from the young cowboys, all of whom wanted to be filled in on the case he was working on.

Chapter 22

Ah, those tits. Magnificent. Huge and soft and pale. Blue-veined and pink-tipped. And warm. Oh, yes, they were warm.

She bent low over him. Smiled. Used her hands to press her tits tight on either side of his stiff cock. Smiled even more as he began slowly stroking up and down, his erection sliding between the sweat-slick mounds. That was good, but it got even better when she dipped her head and opened her mouth so that at the end of each stroke he penetrated, just barely, between her moist and waiting lips.

She was something, this redhead. Her hair spilled in bright copper coils that framed perfect features.

He knew her from . . . he couldn't remember. Her name was . . . dammit, he couldn't bring that to mind either.

But she was beautiful. Big and buxom and as randy as a goat.

And those tits. Fantastic.

The redhead nibbled gently at the tip of his cock, then lifted her chin and smiled at him. She gave him a wink and opened her mouth to speak.

"Marshal. Marshal, sir? D'you want hot water to shave with this morning, sir?"

Longarm frowned. He opened his eyes and sent one peeved glare in the direction of the hotel room door, outside of which the young Jennison was hawking hot water, then another angry glance toward the front wall, where frost coated the wallpaper a dull and ugly white.

The room was frigid, dammit. His ears and the tip of his nose burned with cold despite the heavy blankets that were drawn high beneath his chin, and when he exhaled, his breath was clearly visible in the air. And that was indoors, dammit. He could just imagine what it must be like outside right now.

"Marshal, sir?"

Longarm sighed. "I hear you, son. Yeah, I'll have some of that water. Just a minute."

Longarm steeled himself against the chill that would envelop him as soon as he pushed the covers back—he'd been a helluva lot more comfortable while dreaming about that redhead—and forced himself to do what had to be done.

One nice thing, though. The hard-on that his dream created was no match for the shock of sudden cold that greeted him once he was out from under the blankets. By the time he got to the door to let the kid bring his shaving water in, the flagpole had subsided and Longarm no longer had to worry about embarrassing himself in that manner.

Longarm yawned and stood back while Jim Jennison Junior poured him a generous measure of steaming water. Then Longarm yawned again and reached first for the loose change he'd tossed onto the bedside table, and next for his strop and razor.

"Good morning, sir," the boy said, accepting the nickel tip Longarm handed him.

"It's mornin' anyway," Longarm reluctantly agreed. He wasn't so damn sure about it being any sort of "good."

The boy grinned. "Hotcakes and ham for breakfast today, Marshal."

"I can't hardly wait," Longarm groaned. He dipped his shaving brush into the hot water and began working up a soapy lather in his mug.

"Can I ask you something, Marshal?"

"Go ahead, son." Longarm splashed some water onto his cheeks, enjoying the heat it imparted, and commenced lathering up.

"It's about, you know, that hoor Old Man Travis killed?"

"First off, Jim, that wasn't just a whore that died, it was a girl. She had a family somewhere. Secondly, Mr. Travis wasn't the one that killed her. He was already gone from home when she was taken there and murdered. So . . . what's your question now?"

"I was just . . . I mean . . . she really was one of them . . . you know."

"Whore? Yes, son, she was that."

"She didn't look . . . I mean, I seen her around town a couple times. On the days those women are allowed to shop. You know?"

Longarm nodded. He leaned close to the mirror hung on a carpet tack above the washstand, used his thumb to wipe away some excess lather, and lightly drew the edge of the razor over his flesh. He managed to bring away a swath of lather dotted with flecks of beard stubble. And no blood was left behind. So far so good.

"She was pretty," Jim said.

"That she was, son."

"And not so awful old."

"Not much older than you," Longarm agreed.

"Well, what I was wondering . . . was who killed her."

Longarm paused in the middle of shaving the shelf beneath his jaw. He looked closely at the boy, then smiled. "Tell you what, Jim. I'll answer both your questions."

"Sir?"

"The one you said out loud and the one you really wanted to ask but couldn't quite."

"I don't know what you, uh . . ."

"It's all right. I won't mention this conversation to your folks. Now, as for the question you asked me a minute ago, I don't know yet who killed that girl. I'm sure Mr. Travis did not. As for who did"—he shrugged—"I'll find that out sooner or later. Count on it." Longarm carefully slid the razor up his throat, again without cutting himself, and wiped the blade. He grinned down at the youngster. "As for what you're scared to come right out and ask, that pretty girl prob'ly cost a dollar and a half, maybe two dollars. But son, don't be in too all-fired a hurry to grow up. You hear me? Growing up ain't always as grand as it might seem. Give yourself time and let things come natural."

The kid blushed a furious shade of red and backed away a couple steps. "I didn't mean . . ."

"Of course you didn't. And you'd best go on now before the rest of that water gets cold. I'm sure there's other gentlemen needing their water hot on a morning like this one."

"Yes, sir. Good-bye, sir."

Longarm chuckled a little as he turned back to the mirror and leaned close to concentrate on his shaving.

Chapter 23

"I'd give a dollar for an egg."

"Dollar, hell, I'd give ten."

"Ten?"

"All right, so maybe that's stretching the truth. But I'd beat your dollar if the bidding got started."

Longarm felt pretty much the same as his dining companions, one of them an engineer from the Comstock on his way home to visit relatives and the other a dry goods salesman from Ohio. The difference was that Longarm didn't have money to squander on luxuries like eggs.

And wasn't it saying something odd when you got to thinking about an ordinary egg as a luxury item. Still, the kitchen help at the Jennison Arms swore there wasn't an egg in Kittstown. The storm kept any freight from moving in or out of town, and apparently the few backyard hens in town had stopped laying in the continuing cold and wind.

There was no telling how long the other foodstuffs would hold out. All the fresh meat that the hotel had had on hand at the beginning of the storm was used up and gone now. Breakfast had consisted of hotcakes and fried ham. Longarm hoped for a break in the weather so there would not be the danger of hoarding and food piracy.

Yet at the same time he had to acknowledge that the storm in a way was doing him a favor. It made damn sure the heavy-fisted killer was still in town.

Longarm wadded his napkin into a ball and dropped it beside his plate, adding a nickel tip even though the meal was paid for as part of his lodging.

"In a hurry, Marshal?" the engineer said. "Surely you don't think we're going anywhere today."

"No, I reckon we're here for a spell yet, but I have work to do. Thanks for sharing your table, gents." He stood and took down his coat and fur hat from the rack, bundling up in preparation for the assault of the wind outside.

His first stop was at the railroad depot. The telegraph office was closed. There was no sign of the operator. A small sign propped against the inside of the glass on the door said the telegrapher would be back in fifteen minutes. Longarm rather doubted that considering that when he peered inside he could see the door to the stove standing open ready for a fresh fire to be laid. The telegrapher hadn't come to work yet this morning. And might not be inclined to make it in at all on a day like this one.

Longarm hunched a little deeper inside his coat and trudged off, head down and hands stuffed in his pockets, to his next stop.

"You," Ira Parminter said, not sounding particularly welcoming about it.

"That's right, Mayor, me again."

"What do you want this time?"

"Advice," Longarm said.

110

"Good. I advise you to drop this investigation and leave us alone."

"That isn't exactly what I had in mind," Longarm admitted.

"Pity. So what is it you do want?"

"I need to know who your undertaker is."

"Undertaker? You haven't . . . I mean . . ."

"Have I gone and killed any of your citizens? No. Not yet anyhow. No, I want to make arrangements for the girl's body to be taken care of."

"If you think the town is going to pay for—"

"I'll pay for it my own self," Longarm put in. "It just bothers me to think of her laying out there in that cabin all naked and frozen stiff and bunches of pimple-faced little pieces of shit coming by to stare at her and maybe touch her, God knows what else. Leave her lying there, the little sons of bitches will be having circle jerks around the corpse before the next thaw. I'll sleep better if I know she's safe in a coffin ready to be carried back to her people."

"She was a whore. What if her people don't want her back?"

"Then I'll see she's buried."

"She really got to you, didn't she?" Parminter said. "I wouldn't have thought . . ."

"You wouldn't have thought what?" Longarm demanded when the mayor failed to complete his sentence.

"Never mind."

"Fine. So where can I find your local undertaker."

"Our barber handles that. Do you know where his place is?"

Longarm shook his head, and Parminter gave directions. It wasn't far.

"Anything else?" Parminter asked.

"I could use some of those cheroots."

"Sorry. I'm sold out. No, don't look at me like that. I'm not refusing to do business with you. I'm sold out of half a dozen things that people have started stocking up on. Not just tobacco either. Matches. Lamp oil. Tinned meats and peaches and tomatoes. A couple other things as well. It's strange the way folks have begun to worry all of a sudden. Like they think this wind will never quit."

"This end of Wyoming has a reputation for wind," Longarm said.

"Totally undeserved too." The mayor grinned. "I can remember an afternoon in August not three years back when the wind died off completely and didn't start up again for three or maybe four hours."

"Look, thanks for the directions. And the other advice too. Not that I can take it. But I do understand your problem. If I can avoid making it worse, I will. Is that good enough?"

"I expect it will have to be, won't it."

"Yes, sir, I expect that it will. Good day, Mr. Mayor." Longarm touched a finger to the front of his cap by way of salute and went back out into the biting cut of the wind.

Chapter 24

Two blocks down, one block over. Finding it was easy.
Getting there on the other hand . . .

Longarm was going into the wind most of the way.
He felt like he was swimming in saltwater taffy, having
to push and strain for every foot of progress. He huffed
and struggled and stayed as close as possible to the
buildings he passed, then briefly thought he wasn't going
to make it at all when he had to traverse the open in-
tersections between business blocks.

Still, he did get there eventually, plastered so thick
with the wet, heavy snow that he more closely resembled
a kid's snowman than a walking, talking human being.
Longarm was quite frankly amazed to discover the barbershop door unlocked. Only a crazy person would vol-
untarily go out in shit like this. And no, he did not
exempt himself from that description. Apparently,
though, the barber, like the mayor, had living quarters
attached to his place of work. Damned convenient,
Longarm figured, although with no jealousy whatsoever.

"Shave and a trim for you, mister?" the barber called
from a reclining position in his own chair. Business on

a day like this was perhaps understandably slack.

"It isn't your barbering that I need today," Longarm said.

The barber sat up and leaned forward to peer closely at his customer, squinting in thought as he did so. After a moment, a light of comprehension showed in his bright blues. "You must be the deputy marshal caught in the layover from that train," he said aloud. "Which means you came to see me about that little dead trollop everyone says you're investigating."

"You got it right, friend. Do you know anything about her?"

"I know she had a soft voice and she laughed easy. I liked the sound of it when Nancy laughed."

"You knew her then?"

"Sure. A good many of us in Kittstown liked the way that little girl looked. Enough to choose her out once the money was paid and the fun was about to start. I was with her twice myself, and would've used her again from time to time. Like I said, she was all right. Not the best I've ever had in the sheets, maybe, but nice. I liked her. Damn sure was sorry to hear someone killed her."

"You're honest enough about using her."

"Like I said, Marshal, I liked the girl. It'd please me to see you catch whoever killed her. As for admitting that I go over to Norma's place a couple times every week, why not. I'm not married and not beholden to anyone. Not ashamed of anything I do neither. If I can't stand for all the world to know about it, then I expect I shouldn't do it. And don't. And I flat don't give a damn who knows about my nights with Norma and her young ladies of the evening."

"I wonder if all the gents in town would feel that way about it," Longarm asked.

The barber/undertaker laughed. "I expect you know the answer to that one already."

"Yes, I suppose I do at that."

It had occurred to Longarm before now that he might have to resort to trying to run down all the customers Nancy had had while she was in Kittstown. That would not be an easy thing to accomplish, though. And it would damn sure stir up the reform crowd that the mayor was so worried about. He hoped there would prove to be a better way.

"I don't suppose you know of anything that could help me find the answer to who the killer is," Longarm said.

"No, sir, not that I know of. But if I think of anything I'll come running."

"Yeah, well, in the meantime you can help me by getting her body moved over here just as quick as possible."

"There's really no hurry about that, Marshal. Ira said the inside of Darby's cabin is as cold as an icehouse in January. The girl will keep just fine where she is."

Longarm shook his head. And explained about the problem of the horny young boys who would likely persist in sneaking out there to get a look at a naked, dead whore.

"I hadn't thought of that," the undertaker allowed. "Not that it would do the boys any real hurt. But it isn't dignified. Nancy deserved better. Besides, those boys' mamas get wind of what's going on out at that cabin and there will be hell to pay about sin and wickedness amongst us. Those of us who like a little Saturday night comfort don't want a fuss raised like that."

It was an argument in favor of quick retrieval of the body that Longarm hadn't thought of. But it was certainly a valid one and one that would please the mayor.

"Can you bring her in today?"

The barber frowned. Then he sighed and reluctantly nodded. "I'll have to borrow Ed Turner's sled. I don't have one myself. Got runners that I can fit to my hearse to make it a sleigh, but you'd play hell trying to get a mule to go out in this weather. Better I get hold of Ed's little sled and use that. Can you help me load her onto it?"

"I can do that," Longarm agreed.

"We can go now if you like. I'll just have to change my clothes into something good and warm, then go find Ed and ask him for the use of his delivery sled."

"I tell you what," Longarm suggested. "I need to stop at the telegraph office, so why don't I do that while you're taking care of whatever-all you have to do. I'll get my business out of the way and meet you at Travis's shack. I take it you know the way."

"Surely do, Marshal. Darby Travis is a bachelor too, you see. He and I have spent many a night out there at his place playing chess or dealing hands of rummy. And as often we've gathered here under this roof too, Darby and me and a few of the other crotchety old farts in town. Not so much fun as going over to Norma's, of course, but a sight less expensive. Anyway, that sounds just fine. You go on and do whatever you have to. I'll meet you at Darby's in, oh, say, an hour or thereabouts. Is that long enough for you?"

"Just fine, thanks." Longarm went back out into the storm. He was halfway to the railroad depot when it occurred to him that he hadn't ever gotten the barber's name. Nice fellow, though.

Going with the wind on his way back, Longarm practically flew down the deserted streets. If he'd had boards to slide on, he figured he could have spread his coat wide and sailed the rest of the way. As it was, he made mighty good time despite the lousy conditions.

Chapter 25

Damn telegraph operator still wasn't in. The office was cold and dark. Longarm could have gone inside and opened the key himself. He was more than capable. But he could not honestly claim that this was an emergency. What it was was a nuisance, but that did not give him license to break and enter. God knows he was taking liberties enough by assuming jurisdiction in the girl's death. That sort of thing Billy Vail would let slide should the mayor or anyone else in Kittstown complain. But breaking into the telegraph office might be seen as an excessive sort of zeal and make Billy mad. Longarm just hated it when the boss got all huffy and red in the face.

Of course, the thing that was really peeving him here was that he'd come back all this way in the wind and the snow and accomplished not a damn thing by it. Now he had to turn around and head back into the wind again so he could meet the undertaker at Darby Travis's shack.

There wasn't much for it, he supposed, but to go ahead and get it done. He took a moment to step into a recessed doorway so as to get out of the full force of the wind while he lit a cheroot. Then it was back out into the ball-clanking cold.

Longarm made his way along the storefronts two blocks past the turn toward the barbershop, and recognized the street he wanted by the small, brick bank building on the corner. He braced himself for an instant, squared his shoulders, ducked his head, and stepped out from behind the protection of the bank.

Lordy, it was bitter-nasty. The wind found every gap between his buttons, funneled down the neck of his coat, and likely would have snapped the tip of his nose clean off if he'd blundered head-on into anything solid. Longarm felt frozen right down to the cods, and wasn't sure he would be able to recover from this even if he had a pair of buxom twins and a feather bed to enjoy them in for the next week and a half. Of course in the interests of science he might be willing to *try,* but . . .

He was thinking along those lines, warming himself through the artifice of fancy since there wasn't anything better to hand, when he got himself distracted away from the thoughts of imaginary twins with big tits.

But then the sound of a gunshot has a tendency to do that sort of thing.

The muzzle report sounded thin and hollow on the wind, and wherever the bullet went, it wasn't close enough to be heard over the whine of the gale.

At first Longarm wasn't even sure the shot was intended to come his way.

A second report convinced him.

First there was a faint but unmistakable *thupp* as the bullet sped by to the left of his head, then a louder, wind-distorted sound of a short-barreled gun being fired.

This time Longarm ducked. There was no point, of course. Once you heard the bastard go by, it was already way the hell too late to move aside. Which was one thing

118

to know, but another to convince your body to act upon. The simple truth was that even with flying bullets, a fella was just plain going to duck and never mind the logic of the situation.

Longarm ducked and fumbled inside his coat, cold-numbed fingers groping for the butt of his .44 Colt.

This time he managed, eventually, to get the thing out without ripping any more buttons off. By then he was hunkered low against the wall of a . . . some damn building or other. He had no idea what the place was and didn't much care. His attention at the moment was out in front. Out there where those gunshots came from.

Longarm didn't know where the asshole was. Disgruntled George again? Likely so, he figured. The son of a bitch was hell for persistent. Dumb too, of course. But persistent.

At this point Longarm would quite cheerfully have put a slug into the idiot. If he'd only known where to fire. As for that . . .

Help came in the form of a flash of yellow fire barely visible through the blowing snow.

There was a dark, looming presence out in front of Longarm, maybe fifteen or twenty yards off. And somewhere in the middle of that he saw the muzzle flash of a third gunshot.

The bullet slammed loudly into the hardwood siding that sheathed the building Longarm was leaning against. The sound of it was dull and hollow. Longarm hoped the slug hadn't penetrated the wall and hurt somebody inside.

Longarm snapped a shot of his own in the direction of the muzzle flash and then, while good old George should be busy doing some ducking his own self, scuttled low and fast to his left and then charged straight forward, directly at the spot where the bullets were coming from.

Chapter 26

A solid hit, hard and painful, took Longarm's right leg out from under him. He fell, rolled, ended up half buried in drifted snow. His leg was more numb than not. He couldn't see any blood, couldn't tell if the leg was broken, didn't have enough feeling above the combined numbness of cold and injury to decide, couldn't tell how much damage the slug had done or . . . slug? It occurred to him that he'd neither heard a shot nor seen a muzzle flash. So why the hell not?

He quit staring toward the tall, gray building where the gunman was, and looked back to where he'd been running when he went down.

Shit! He hadn't been shot. He'd run straight into the side of a water trough lying low to the ground and almost completely buried by the snow. That was what had taken his leg out from under him. All he had wrong with him was a hard whack on the shin. Which didn't make it hurt any less, but was not altogether bad news, considering.

Longarm rubbed his leg and climbed back onto his feet, heading out again at a brisk limp.

It was a water trough he'd fallen over. And now he was close enough to recognize the profile of the tall building in front of him. Apparently George was holed up inside the Kittstown livery barn. Longarm had passed the place a number of times before, although he'd never had occasion to enter it in the past.

No time like the present, he decided. He dropped to the ground to study the structure in front of him.

There was the usual set of large sliding doors paired at the front of the place to give access into the customary center aisle, where feed wagons could be drawn through and where teams of horses could be harnessed indoors when the weather was bad.

Probably there would be a work area to one side of the entry and an office and/or tack room on the other. Back of those and on either side of the aisle there should be stalls where horses or mules could be kept. And overhead there should be a loft for the storage of hay, and perhaps feed grain in bins as well.

That, however, was guesswork based on what was common and ordinary. Longarm wished to hell he knew for certain sure what the layout of this particular barn would prove to be.

One thing he was sure of, though. He did not intend to waltz up to those double doors and let himself in through them. No, thank you. If George still was anywhere inside, he would have Longarm silhouetted clean against the thin daylight and be able to put a slug into his belly with no trouble at all. Longarm figured he could get along just fine without that sort of welcome. He would just have to find another way in.

Since he happened to be on the ground anyway, he took that as a good suggestion and stayed low, holding the muzzle of his revolver out of the snow and crawling off to the side so as to avoid being seen from the doorway. Or wherever the hell George was hiding.

He reached the rails of one of the corrals and slipped through them. Using the solid wood of a feed bunk to shield him from view—and from bullets if it came to that—he approached the side wall of the tall barn.

Damn a man who would design a building without windows, Longarm thought. Still, there had to be a way in. Better yet, there had to be a *safe* way in.

With no access at ground level, he figured he would have to try elsewhere. Like through the loft. Normally there were loading doors at the front and rear where block and tackle could be used to lift baled hay or sacked grain into the loft and where hay could be tossed down to ground level for feeding in the corrals. Surely there was such an arrangement here. If he could only get to it.

Longarm made his way to the back of the barn, his leg still hurting like fire but continuing to respond to the demands he made of it. He could see the shutter-like hayloft doors high on the back wall. The back-end barn doors, a matching pair to the big ones up front, were tightly closed, which meant George could neither slip out of them himself without exposing himself to Longarm's fire, nor see what was going on outdoors. That was to the good. But how the hell was Longarm going to reach a pair of doors at the second-story level when he had no ladder to use.

Where there was a will there was a way, he thought. And all that good crap.

If you don't have what you want, then use what you have. He went back around the side of the barn and took a firm grip on the hay bunk there. He tugged and pushed at it a few times. And was relieved to feel the contraption rock back and forth on its skids. The bunk was not, thank goodness, frozen to the earth. There'd been plenty of cold, but not enough daytime sun or warming of temperatures to start any melting. The unrelenting bitterness of the cold was what had prevented any slight thaw that would have refrozen and attached the bunk solidly to the earth. Thus, the hay bunk could be moved.

Longarm put a shoulder to it and commenced pushing, bad leg and all. It hurt like hell, but it was a thing that had to be done. Once he overcame the initial resistance and got the hay bunk sliding, it was fairly easy to sled it across the frozen earth and around the corner to the yard at the back of the barn.

There he took a firm grip on one end and lifted, straining. He tipped the hay bunk on end. Immediately beneath the hayloft doors.

Then, quickly, he began to climb. Scaling the side of the upended bunk, he stood on what should have been one end of the feed trough and was able to reach the loft doors. He pulled, hard, and the door swung open on rusted hinges.

Now if only George was concentrating on the possible entry points at ground level and had not thought to climb into the loft to wait . . .

Chapter 27

It was a mite nervous-making. Longarm needed both hands to climb into the loft. Which meant shoving the .44 Colt back into its holster. Which meant if ol' George was in there waiting, then Longarm was up the proverbial creek with not even a glimpse of a paddle.

Still, there wasn't anything to gain by waiting, especially since Longarm's balance atop the upended hay bunk was shaky at best. Quickly, before he had time to think of all the things that could go wrong with this move, he dragged the door open, took a grip on the ragged floorboards, and hauled himself bodily into the dark opening.

He scrambled inside, rolled once to his right, and came up onto a knee with the Colt once more in his fist.

All he lacked now was a target.

It took a moment for his eyes to adjust to the relative darkness inside the loft. Loose hay was piled to the ceiling save for a V-shaped path down the middle of the loft where a man could walk through.

Longarm walked through, moving as quietly as he could between the walls of clean, sweet-smelling hay on either side of him.

124

Toward the middle of the barn he could see a ladder and trapdoor leading down to the ground floor. The hay was less solidly piled in an arc around the ladder, obviously the result of some of the fodder having been forked down to the livestock below.

On the far side of the trapdoor he could see some large bins, presumably containing oats, shelled corn, or other such feed grains for use through the winter. There seemed to be a hopper arrangement built into the grain bins that would allow grain to be dropped down a chute to ground level for mixing and feeding. All very modern and scientific, he was sure.

Of course from Longarm's point of view, the only thing of consequence here was the question of exactly where George was hiding.

Packed as the hayloft was, Longarm was reasonably sure no one was lurking on this second-story level.

Which meant he was going to have to quit hanging back and get on with doing what had to be done. In this case that meant moseying on over to that trapdoor and sticking his head into the opening so he could get a look at what-all was going on below.

The prospect was not especially inviting.

Still, all George had let loose at him so far was a small-caliber revolver. And not one the man was particularly accurate with. Longarm tried to find some comfort in those two facts. Damn near did too. Then he realized what a wonderful joke it would be on him if someone as inept as George managed to nail him with a pea-shooter like that little pocket gun the man carried.

Funny? Enough to make a man spit.

Longarm stretched himself belly-down on the loose, slippery hay that had spilled into the walkway, and slithered forward toward the gaping trapdoor.

He was perhaps a foot and a half from it when the

gent below apparently heard the loft floorboards creak and groan under Longarm's weight. That or some other sound tipped the ambusher to the danger above, and the son of a bitch went and did something about it.

With a shotgun, dammit, and not the little bitty noise-maker he'd been using up until now.

The scattergun went off with a roar, and a charge of heavy shot came tearing through the floor close enough in front of Longarm's nose to fill his mustache with splinters. Helluva way for a man to get a trim.

Longarm jerked back involuntarily and rolled, that part of it deliberate, quickly to his left.

Down below the second barrel bellowed, and a hole the size of a demitasse saucer was punched out of the floor. More splinters rained down, but Longarm wasn't paying any mind to them.

The shotgun pretty much had to be empty for the moment. Which was the way Longarm liked those things best. Temporarily useless. Damn right.

He quit moving left and hurled himself forward. He grabbed a ladder rung and let himself down hand-over-hand, hitting every second or third rung and moving fast and just barely under control as he dropped.

He heard the telltale *ca-chunk* of metal locking against metal as the shotgun tubes snapped shut over fresh shells. Time to move. Right-damn-NOW!

He was still four or five feet high on the ladder, but didn't take time for an exact measurement. He pushed himself away from the ladder and ducked his shoulder as he hit the packed earth of the livery barn floor, rolling as he did so and diving for the protection of a stall. The fact that that particular stall was already occupied seemed unimportant at the time. Longarm slid underneath the bottom rail scant fractions of a second ahead of a charge of shotgun pellets.

The noise and stink of the gunshots did nothing to promote tranquillity among the barn's residents. The stall where Longarm was lying housed a brown and white paint horse with a milky left eye and a mean disposition. The sonuvabitch tried to kick Longarm.

Longarm rolled out of the way, in the process winding up half out of the stall and at least partially exposed to view by anyone standing in the alley. The natural consequence was that he was rewarded with another roar from the shotgun.

"God*dammit!*"

Longarm rolled back into the stall. The paint took another swipe at Longarm's head, its manure-packed hoof coming uncomfortably close.

That did it. Longarm jumped to his feet and kicked the paint in the belly. "Get, damn you." The horse got. As far, at least, as the far corner of its stall, where it stood trembling, obviously scared shitless by the shotgun blasts. Longarm couldn't actually say that he blamed the animal. Shotguns didn't do a hell of a lot for his peace of mind either.

Ignoring the horse, he paused for a moment to glance at his Colt. Just to make sure he hadn't gone and stuffed the muzzle into a pile of fresh shit or something while he was busy wallowing around on the floor. Plugging up a gun barrel could ruin a man's whole day.

Not that he would mind, particularly, if the asshole at the other end of the barn wanted to plug his barrels and give the triggers a yank. Longarm rather wished that he would.

By now George had had time to reload again.

Longarm debated diving over the top of the wall separating this stall from the next one down the line. But he didn't see that that would accomplish much.

Unfortunately, the walls between the stalls were solid.

127

Only those facing onto the aisle had rails that a man could go under or through.

But then, to look on the bright side of things, it was the fact that he was behind a solid wall that was shielding him from good old George and his scattergun. You get a little, you give a little. And things could have been worse.

The way Longarm figured it, he had George trapped in that far end of the barn. George couldn't get out any easier than Longarm could have gotten in at ground level. There were no windows down at that end of the building, and Longarm could see the tops of the sliding double doors. If one of them moved, Longarm would know right where to be aiming when he came busting out of the stall.

As for the hayloft, Longarm was between George and the ladder.

No, George had gone and trapped himself. There was no getting around that.

And time was definitely on Longarm's side. Hell, he could afford to wait right where he was until Hell, as well as Kittstown, froze over if that was what it took.

After all, he was not the one who needed to get away.

"Care to give yourself up now?" Longarm called out. "It won't be any easier later on, and you won't have any more choices then than you do right now. Do this the easy way, why don'cha, and throw your guns out where I can see them, then step into the middle of the aisle there with your hands held out to your sides."

Longarm expected some sort of answer from George. That was the polite thing to do.

Instead he heard not a word from down at that end of the barn, just a little stomping and whinnying from the occupants of the stalls down that way.

In another minute or so Longarm understood why it was that the natives were getting restless.

After a minute or so Longarm could smell the sharp and distinctive—and damn well ugly—odor of smoke beginning to fill the cold air inside the livery stable.

And if there was anything more to be feared inside a barn than fire, Longarm didn't know what the hell it might be.

He cursed loudly and threw the stall door open, driving the paint horse out into the aisle in front of him.

Chapter 28

Longarm hunched his shoulders, expecting at any moment to hear—and to feel—the blast of a shotgun. But all he heard were the cries of terrified horses and mules and, not as loud but far more ominous, the intensifying crackle and roar of the fire.

He threw the front doors open, and the paint horse practically bowled him over as it rushed into the cold freedom outside.

Longarm regained his balance and dashed back to the row of stalls, throwing the latches and swinging doors open as rapidly as he could.

The animals were frightened, but not yet beyond reason. As soon as their way was clear they galloped for safety.

Longarm was halfway down the aisle, and had just released a pair of sleek mules into the open, when he realized that the double doors at the back of the barn were also open and that the first few sets of stalls there had been emptied.

Longarm could hardly believe it. That bastard George had struck him as a city sort through and through. Yet after setting a disastrous fire, the bastard had taken time to free the animals at that end of the barn before making his own escape. That was not the sort of thing Longarm would have expected from him. But then nerve enough to come hunting for a federal peace officer was not really behavior Longarm would have expected out of George either.

George. Was that his right name? Or was it Harry. The miserable blowhard was such an ineffectual piece of shit that Longarm couldn't remember which was the man's name and which was the moniker Longarm had been ragging him with. Not that it mattered. Not while he was standing inside a barn that all of a sudden had turned into a raging conflagration.

The last of the animals were out, and it was damn sure time for Longarm to turn tail as well. The fire had reached the dry hay piled thick in the loft overhead, and at this point there wasn't a prayer that the barn or any part of it could be saved.

Now the concern would have to be for all the structures downwind of the livery.

If those caught fire, a quarter, maybe a third of Kittstown could be lost.

Longarm spun on his heels and raced out of the barn scant seconds behind the last mule. George had gone out the other end. There was no point in looking for him now.

Besides, as long as this storm lasted there was no way George could leave town. Longarm would be able to find him when he really wanted the asshole.

Now the idea was to keep the livery fire from enveloping the adjacent city blocks.

Longarm was relieved to see that some of the townspeople were already alerted to the danger. Men and boys and even a few women were already on the street carrying blankets and brooms and shovels, anything at hand that they could use to beat out wind-borne embers or dowse them with snow to keep new fires from starting.

Ira Parminter was there, and a good many other shop-keepers. Longarm recognized a surprising number of the people who'd turned out in the face of the cold and the blowing snow to fight this threat to the community. Longarm saw Jim Jennison Junior, and the bartender from the Old Heidelberg, and two of the young poker-playing cowboys who liked to hang out there.

Parminter recognized Longarm too, and came running over to him. "There shouldn't have been any way a fire could start in there," he shouted over the combined noises of wind and flame. "Some fool must have been in there trying to keep warm and let his fire get out of hand. Isn't that illegal?"

"I know for a certain-sure fact that the start of this fire was illegal, Mr. Mayor," Longarm agreed.

"In that case, Marshal, I want to invite you to assume jurisdiction and take charge of the investigation. Who-ever started this has to be taught a lesson."

"Glad to oblige," Longarm said. "I'll wire my boss in Denver soon as I find the telegraph office open."

Parminter blushed. It was hard to tell for sure since his face was already red and chapped from the wind. But Longarm was pretty sure the man was blushing. He damn sure seemed uncomfortable about something. Then he blurted out, "In your wire you can, well, tell Marshal Vail to, uh, ignore the message I sent him a little while ago."

"I'll do that," Longarm said. He was careful to re-frain from asking for particulars about what was con-tained in that message. But then he didn't have to. The general tone of it was plainly seen in the mayor's em-barrassment. The details didn't much matter at this point.

"It looks like you folks have things under control here," Longarm said. "Reckon I'll make that visit to the telegraph office. Then see what I can do about putting your arsonist under arrest."

Longarm did not say anything out loud for Parminter to overhear, but the truth was that he was glad he could bring George in on a charge of arson. No sense in adding anything about assault on a federal officer since that would only muddy the waters when it came to Longarm's shaky claims to jurisdiction in the murder case.

And he damn well was not going to give up on that one. Not until some-damn-body was behind bars where he properly belonged. Not until that girl was back with her family, whoever and wherever they were.

Longarm was jolly well adamant on that subject.

Chapter 29

"I don't know what the sonuvabitch's proper name is. George something-or-other." Longarm described the loudmouth, and the clerk manning the Jennison Arms desk nodded.

"That would be Mr. Mabry," the fellow said, "from, if I remember correctly, Ohio. A salesman, I believe."

"Do you happen to know if Mr. Mabry is in?" Longarm asked.

"Oh, yes. I'm quite sure that he is."

"Room number?" Longarm got his directions and took the stairs two at a time to get there. Cocksucker, he was thinking. Try to commit murder, burn down maybe half a town, and now here he was lollygagging in his hotel room like there was nary a thing to be concerned with in the whole damn world. Well, it was time good old George commenced to concern himself with a few things.

Longarm found the room all right, and stopped outside it. No sense taking chances, he decided. George had proved more slippery than Longarm realized back in that barn a little while ago. Longarm didn't want him sneaking out the window, and there was no one Longarm could count on to cover that escape route. Whatever was done here, Longarm was going to have to do it all. Well, so be it.

He drew his Colt and held it ready. He took a deep breath and set himself for a surprise entrance. Then he reared back and kicked the door. Hard. The sole of his boot landed smack beside the knob and the area where the bolt would be placed.

Wood splintered and flew, and the door burst open with a crash.

Longarm, gun leveled and ready to fire, followed the broken door into the room, taking a whack on his shoulder as the door hit the inside wall and rebounded on its hinges. Longarm did not so much as notice.

"Federal officer! Don't move!" he barked.

He needn't have bothered. No one inside seemed inclined to go anywhere.

There were two beds in the cheap room. Each of them was occupied. George Mabry lay in one, bedclothes tucked up high under his chin. His smaller partner, the man who seemed to accompany him most everywhere Mabry went, lay in the other. Both men were in nightshirts. Each appeared to be flushed with high fevers.

"Jesus Christ. You again," Mabry moaned. "What do you want this time?"

"You, asshole. You're under arrest for arson."

"You're kidding me. Aren't you? No, I see that you are not. I haven't done anything. I swear I haven't. Tony? Tell him Tony. Tell him I haven't . . . arson, you say? Why would I do that? Where?"

"You know damn good and well what you did and why."

"Would you tell me when I'm supposed to have burned whatever you say I burned, Long?"

135

"You admit that you know who I am now."

"Of course I do. I asked about you yesterday after that incident in the saloon. You embarrassed me. As soon as I'm able to go out again, let me tell you, I intend to file a complaint with your employer."

"I'll write down his name and address for you. But in the meantime, Mabry, you're under arrest for arson. I might want to add attempted murder to that later on. And probably assault on a federal officer."

Mabry groaned.

"Get up. I'm taking you to jail, Harry. And believe me, it will be a pleasure."

"I can't get up. Jesus. Leave me be, will you?"

"Tough shit. Now get outa that bed and turn around so I can put some cuffs on you."

"Look, dammit, I'm sick. I've been up and down all night and all morning with fever and diarrhea. I feel like I'm going to die. Every muscle and joint I have is aching. Come back and arrest me tomorrow if you like. I'm not going anywhere. No one is. Not until this storm lets up."

"Marshal," the other man said.

"Yes?"

"George and me both have been sick all through the night. If you think he did anything, or me either, from about ten o'clock last night on, check with the people here in the hotel. They've had to change our chamber pots every hour or so all through the night and all this morning. Neither one of us has been able to hold any food down. I don't know what we got, tainted food or whatever, but it's got the both of us down. Don't take my word for that. Ask them down at the desk. They know we've been here right along."

"Since ten last night?" Longarm asked. "Neither one of you was out this morning?"

136

"Neither one of us has been able to sit up, much less stand on his own two feet. Not since last night. Ask them. Ask the boy. Jimmy, is it? He's been doing for us since early this morning when he came around with the hot water. Ask him."

"Don't think I won't," Longarm said.

"Listen, I hope you will. Really. George does too. And Marshal."

"Yes?"

"Don't judge George too harshly. He blusters and carries on sometimes, but he's really a good fellow. Honestly."

Longarm scowled. But he put his gun away. There was no doubt that both men in this room were sick. He could see it. For that matter, he could smell it. The interior of the room had that dank, sour stench of puke and fever. And no one, not the finest actor, could likely fake the flushed and sweaty look that George had on his ugly face.

But if both these men really hadn't left their room today—which Longarm would damn well check with Jim Jennison Junior and the other employees of the hotel—*then who the hell had been shooting at Longarm lately? And why?*

He turned and rather reluctantly retreated through the shattered door.

Dammit, he grumbled to himself. He wondered if he could slip the damages for that door past Billy Vail's clerk Henry when Longarm made out his expense voucher for this trip.

Chapter 30

For a change the telegraph operator was in and available for business. Longarm wrote out his messages and sent them, billing the charges to the United States Department of Justice.

Then once again he went shivering back into the teeth of the storm.

By now it was much too late to meet the barber/undertaker at Darby Travis's cabin, so Longarm looked for him at the barbershop as before.

The door was unlocked, although there was no sign of life in the shop. Once inside, however, Longarm could hear sounds of someone stirring around in a back room.

"Hello. Is anybody here?"

The barber came out, his shirt sleeves rolled to his elbows and a smile on his face. The shirt cuffs stayed where they were, but when he saw who the visitor was, his expression fell on the double quick. "Oh. It's you."

"Sorry, but someone tried to shoot me on my way to meet you." Longarm shrugged. "It's what you might call an occupational hazard."

"Did you hear the livery burned down?"

"Yeah, I did."

"Someone really shot at you?"

"Is your concern professional? Or personal?"

The barber grinned just a little. "So maybe business hasn't been all that great lately."

"I'll let you give me a haircut if it will help out, but I draw the line at volunteering for your other services."

The barber's grin got bigger. "Speaking of which, and no help from you, I might add, I got the girl loaded onto the sled and brought her back. I was starting to work on her just now."

"Good."

"Incidentally, it was a good thing you made me get out there when you did. There were some kids in the cabin, just like before. They had the covers off her and were doing God knows what before I got there and scared them away. Probably having a circle jerk, the little bastards. Fortunately, I know who they are. I'll tell their daddies, and I can pretty much promise you that those boys will be making some woodshed visits. And taking their meals off their mantels for a while."

"You can't blame them, I suppose," Longarm allowed. "God knows I was a horny little shit my own self when I was young. But you can't let it go on either. It isn't right, never mind what Nancy did for a living."

"Come on into the back if you like," the barber offered. From the way he said it, with an exaggerated normalcy that suggested a shyness that the man would rather not admit to, Longarm suspected it was highly unusual for anyone to be invited to look in on that side of his livelihood. A professional courtesy perhaps, acknowledging Longarm's livelihood, which also dealt with death?

Naw, probably not. He was just reading stuff in where

it didn't belong. "Glad to," was all he said, and the barber led the way.

The room was small and kept toasty warm with a coal-burning stove. Nancy's slim, pale form was laid out on a broad, very heavy table.

"I built the fire high so she'll thaw out," the man said. "She has to be thawed completely or I can't pump the embalming fluid through the arteries."

"I thought you wouldn't have to embalm her. I thought you'd just use a lead-sealed coffin and send her the way she was."

The undertaker gave Longarm a sheepish look. "When I saw her like this . . . I don't know that I can explain it. But . . . I didn't want anything more to happen to her to . . . well, to take any more dignity away from her. If you know what I mean."

"I know," Longarm said in a small voice.

"She had . . . maybe I shouldn't be telling you this, but if you think I'm a fool because of it, so be it . . . the thing is, when I was trying to pick her up and get her out to the sled, the light was slanting across her cheek and I saw . . . what I saw was a tear, frozen there on her flesh. It may sound silly, but when I saw that . . ."

"I saw it too, friend. That's why I want so bad to find out who killed her."

"You do understand what I mean then."

"Yeah," Longarm said. "I surely do."

The undertaker cleared his throat. Then smiled. "You concentrate on doing your job, Marshal. I'll do mine. I'll embalm her the very best I know how and put her in the best coffin I have. Then I'll let that stove go out and keep her safe here as long as need be. Whenever there's a train ready to carry her . . . and once you decide where you want to take her . . . I'll have her ready to travel."

"Do whatever you think best, my friend, and give me the bill."

The undertaker shook his head. "Not this time. No charge. I . . . just consider it a gift from me to a girl I kinda think of as a friend."

"I tell you what, then," Longarm said. "Let's you and me split the bill."

"I can go along with that."

Longarm sighed and walked across the room. He stood over the dead girl, looking down on the undamaged and still quite lovely side of her young and pretty face.

She had been something, this child of sorrow and pain. And whatever she might have done in the past, she never deserved to end up here on a wooden slab far from her family and those who loved her.

The tear was still there, he saw. The tear that affected him and that likewise affected the Kittstown undertaker.

It was thawing now, that tear, the ice turning soft and commencing to sag lower on her cheek.

On an impulse Longarm collected the bit of moisture on the ball of his thumb and, before he consciously gave thought to it, tasted of its tart and salty flavor.

The gesture was a vow of sorts, a taking into himself of something of this dead and abused girl-child.

Whoever had done this to her had done it also to him.

And for that there could be no mercy.

"Reckon I'd best get to work now," Longarm said, "and leave you to yours."

"If there is anything I can do . . ."

"I'll call on you. And thanks." Longarm gave Nancy one last look, then spun on his heels and strode out to face the storm and whatever else might be hidden inside the white curtain of blowing snow.

Chapter 31

He wasn't sure, but when he went outside he thought the wind had let up just a little. Maybe.

Still cold as a witch's tit, though. Still blowing snow. But maybe just the least little bit less snow moving around in the air. Visibility seemed a tiny bit better. If there was anything they needed, it was a break in the weather. To get the trains moving again. To get some food stocks and other things coming in again. Those things were sorely needed.

On the other hand, once the railroad tracks were open Nancy's killer, or killers, would be free to leave Kittstown. And if there was anything Custis Long did not want, it would be for him/them to get away. That was just plainly not acceptable.

He tugged his fur hat low and turned his coat collar high, and made his way almost comfortably back toward town.

The livery stable was gone, he saw. Charred beams and black rubble, not a stick of any of it standing more than waist high, were all that was left. The snow downwind from where the barn had stood was gray from windswept ash and soot, but he was pleased to see that the townspeople had been able to keep the adjacent buildings from catching fire. The only damage was to the livery. And that could be rebuilt if the owner wanted. The corrals were intact and the well would still be good. A couple of hayricks had burned down with the barn, and of course whatever tack and feeds were stored inside. For the sake of the innocent owner of the business, Longarm hoped he'd been well insured against fire loss.

Longarm hurried on by and turned down the main street toward the mayor's general mercantile.

Perhaps because the excitement of the fire had forced so many people outdoors, the store was busy. Longarm couldn't recall seeing anyone else in the place on his previous visits, but now there were several ladies and three men browsing through the merchandise.

None of them seemed to be having much luck finding the things they wanted.

"I'm sorry, Mrs. Corbett," Parminter was saying to a buxom matron with a bun so tight the corners of her eyes were pulled back to make her look Chinese. "We don't have any meats at all, not even bacon. No wheat flour, no tinned fruits, and no sugar left either. I still have some cornmeal and a good supply of rice. Still have some raisins and plenty of that awful pemmican I was foolish enough to buy off a passing Shoshone a while back. Oh, yes. I still have near a whole crock of sauerkraut. I keep forgetting about that. But then it smells so bad that I keep it in the storeroom and never think to mention it."

"How much cornmeal did you say you have, Mr. Parminter?"

"About ten pounds or a little better, Mrs. Corbett."

"I will take it all off your hands, sir. And raisins and some of that rice and—"

"Leandra!" the other lady gasped.

"Something wrong, dear?"

"You could share that cornmeal with me, you know."

"How much do you want, dear?"

"Half."

"I would give up two pounds. No more."

"Half," the other woman insisted. "And the rest of those raisins, Mr. Parminter. And . . ."

The list was impressive. Parminter jotted it all down, added up the ladies' bills, and informed them of the totals. The Corbett woman sniffed and made an imperious little waggle of her finger advising Parminter to put the amount on her account. The other lady pulled out a coin purse and counted out the exact amount for her purchases.

"I'll see your orders are delivered no later than noon tomorrow," the mayor told them.

"Very well. Good day, sir." "Good-bye."

Longarm touched the front of his hat and hurried to hold the door open for them. When he got back to the counter he had to wait in line while a couple of gents made minor purchases of woolen stockings and the like. When the store finally cleared, Longarm observed, "Funny thing about those women that were in here."

"How's that?"

"It's the one that asked for credit that I would've taken for the better off of the two, seeing how they were dressed and everything."

Parminter grunted. "You weren't wrong. Ben Corbett is one of the wealthiest men in this county. Likely in this end of Wyoming, for that matter."

Longarm shook his head. "Then why'd his missus want credit while the poorer one paid cash?"

"Didn't you know? The rich don't need cash. Han-

144

dling it is a nuisance. It's only us poor folks that have to worry about paying up on time."

Longarm chuckled a bit, and would have said something more, but the street door pushed open and four snow-covered figures came tumbling in, bringing a flurry of laughter along with them. Longarm recognized the friendly young cowboys he'd played poker with earlier. "Hello, Billy. Jason. Carl." It took him a moment to remember the fourth one's name. "Ronnie."

"Hello, Marshal. Mr. Mayor." The young men stamped snow off their boots and whipped it from their clothes using the brims of their hats, and in general filled the store with their clatter. "We're needing tobacco, Mr. Parminter." "Matches too," one of them put in. "And some groceries. We need bacon, lard, flour, coffee." "And salt. Don't forget we're about out of salt."

"Sorry, boys, but I'm almost cleaned out."

"Of what?"

"Of everything."

"But you have to have *some* of the stuff we need. Surely you can't be out of it all."

"Sorry. No, wait. I have salt. And let me see what else you might be able to use." Parminter went through his list, and the boys decided on an order that was fairly extensive considering that they likely wouldn't know what to do with most of it.

"We'll take the stuff with us, Mr. Parminter. On tick like usual."

"You're running up a pretty good-sized bill, fellows. Especially for so early in the season. I don't think . . ."

"You know we're good for it, Mr. Parminter."

"Soon as the spring gather starts we'll be drawing pay again."

"We never let you down before."

"I know that, but you've never spent this heavy before either."

"We had a run of bad luck, that's all."

"Some damn sharpies like to cleaned us out a couple weeks ago. A pair of them acting like they didn't know each other."

"They seen us coming and they whipsawed us before we knew what they was up to."

"They left us short for the year."

"But smarter. We won't be taken like that again, Mr. Parminter."

"And you know we wouldn't leave you holding the bag for us, sir. We've always been straight with you before now, haven't we?"

Parminter frowned and pulled at his lip some, but after a few moments he sighed and brought out his accounts book. "I'll mark this down along with the rest. But mind you, don't abuse the privilege."

"Yes, sir." "No, sir, we won't." "We'll take care, sir, honest."

"Wait here while I get some sacks for you to carry your things in."

When the mayor turned his back and stepped into the storeroom, Billy Madlock winked at Longarm and grinned. "Gonna come over to the saloon later and give us some lessons in poker, Marshal?"

"You'll be playing tonight?"

"Hey, we got to make some money somehow. It might as well be yours."

Longarm smiled. "If I can, boys, I might sit in for a few hands."

"You're always welcome. You know that."

The mayor returned and assembled the purchases into four packages. "Mind what I said now," he warned.

"Yes, sir, we will." The boys, grinning and poking

at one another, took their things out into the gathering dusk.

"Where were we?" Parminter asked. "Oh, yes. I was going to ask you about the arsonist. You said earlier that you had a line on him. May I assume that you've arrested him by now?"

"Yeah, well, um . . ."

Chapter 32

There was something terribly wrong, and it took Longarm half a dozen strides down the middle of the street before he realized just what it was that was so odd here.

It was silent.

For the first time in days, for the first time since they'd all stumbled off that Union Pacific coach and made their way to the Jennison Arms, there was no wind blowing.

None. The air was still and silent.

Oh, the cold was as bad as ever. The snow squeaked beneath his boots with every step he took, and that meant the temperature was either below zero or very near to it.

But without the wind to drive the cold through cloth and deep inside the flesh, even a zero-degree temperature reading felt damn near toasty.

And he could hear what was going on around him. Up the street, in the direction of the Old Heidelberg, Longarm could hear the rattly jangle of a badly played piano. Somewhere inside the narrow alley separating two nearby store buildings he could hear the scratching and whining of a stray dog trying to paw a meal out of the refuse it found there. And from somewhere else, Longarm had no idea where, he heard a child's laughter.

The moan and shriek of a vicious wind were the only sounds of Kittstown he'd had until now. This change was mighty pleasant indeed.

Longarm felt positively jaunty as he tilted the fur hat onto the back of his head—next time he came out he could go back to wearing his favorite Stetson if he liked and the hell with this second-hand soldier-boy affair— and tried to whistle his way along to the railroad depot. But it was simply too damn cold to manage a proper pucker, and his attempts to whistle came off as more of a hiss than a tune. Kind of like blowing out birthday candles in rhythm.

Still, it was almighty comfortable outdoors for a change, and that was enough to boost Longarm's spirits.

He ambled down the middle of the street. The wind had piled deep drifts most everywhere else, so that un-less the shopkeepers had already begun digging paths to their doorways, it was a helluva lot easier to stay far away from walls and buildings, to stay out where the earth had been swept free of snow while the wind was so harsh. Soon he reached the railroad station, hoping by now he might have answers to some of the telegraph messages he'd sent earlier.

No such luck. The telegraph operator was gone again, this time leaving a note saying he would be back at seven in the morning.

Longarm scowled but didn't bother to snarl. After all, there was nothing he could do about it, and complaining would not bring the man back. Nor was there any real emergency that would justify Longarm going off to drag the fellow back to his key. Best just to accept things the way they were and check again in the morning.

In the meantime Longarm celebrated the improvement

149

in the weather by bringing out a cheroot and lighting it. Why, he didn't even have to cup his hands around the match to keep the flame alive. There was no breeze whatsoever.

All day long he'd been hoarding his smokes, holding back whenever he felt the desire to light up because there was no telling how long it might be before fresh supplies began to reach Kittstown.

Now, if the wind remained calm, it looked like the rails should be open again in . . . what? A day or two? Likely, Longarm thought.

The railroad would be more anxious than anyone else to get the line clear and functioning once more. After all, their profits came from what they hauled from one place to another, not from what they had loaded onto idle cars.

As quick as they could punch the plows through, they would be moving freight again. And passengers.

Longarm thought about that for a few moments while he stood in the waning sunlight and savored the taste of his smoke.

People would be able to leave Kittstown by rail again. They could leave right this minute if they wanted to go on horseback and trust that the wind would not resume.

That meant Nancy's killer, or killers, might already be out of reach.

The thought was sufficiently unpleasant to wipe the satisfaction off Longarm's face and bring a tight-knit scowl back.

Dammit, there had to be *some* fucking thing he could do to smoke those killers out.

Killers. Plural. That was how he persisted in thinking of them. There almost had to be more than one of them, he figured. Surely no one man would stay in the ice-house cold of that unheated cabin long enough to be able to repeatedly rape the girl. The sheer volume of semen found on and in her body was enough to convince Longarm that more than one man used her. Took turn and turnabout with her, whether with or without her consent at that moment. And then, for whatever reason, whether from anger or an inability to pay as promised, or simply for the pleasure of causing pain to someone who could not defend herself, when they were finished the sons of bitches killed her.

They. Whoever. And now, dammit, they could get away if they wanted.

Longarm figured he needed to come up with something—he had no idea what—to prevent that from happening.

Damn them!

Chapter 33

"You wanted to see me, sir?"

Longarm looked up from a three-month-old copy of the *Police Gazette* that he'd found lying about in the lobby of the Jennison Arms. He was waiting, with more resignation than relish, for the call to supper. A waiter had already told him what to expect on this day of short supplies and makeshift menus. Supper for everyone would be ham broth and baking powder dumplings. The menu choices were limited: take it or leave it. At least, thank goodness, the price was right; the railroad would be paying for it.

Supper would come shortly, though. At the moment young Jim Jennison Junior was standing there. Longarm had left word at the desk that he wanted to speak with the boy.

"Sit down, Jim. I wanted to ask you about one of the guests here."

"Oh, sir, I can't gossip about—"

"This is official business, son. Not gossip. I already know the answer I expect you'll give, but I have to ask it anyway. It's about George Mabry and his friend. They

152

said you can confirm that they haven't left their room since sometime last night."

The youngster made a sour face. And vouched for Mabry's story. Both men, he said, had been deathly ill the whole night long and all morning too. Neither could possibly have gone outside without someone knowing it. He personally had been in and out of their room half a dozen times or more trying to keep their bedding fresh and the chamber pot emptied. It was not the sort of chore he enjoyed doing.

Once that formality was out of the way, the boy stood to take his leave, but hesitated for a few seconds before doing so. "Can I ask you something, Marshal?"

"Of course, Jim. Ask whatever you like."

"How is your investigation coming into . . . you know."

"The girl Nancy?"

"Yes, sir."

"Not as well as I would like," Longarm admitted. "I can't find anyone who saw or heard a thing, and without that . . ." Longarm shrugged and shook his head.

"Sure is a shame, ain't it, that criminals don't leave a mark when they go and do something rotten like that," the youngster sympathized.

"It surely is," Longarm agreed.

"Well, if you'll excuse me, sir, I have work to do."

"Thanks, son, you've been a big help." Longarm hesitated. Then smiled. And finally laughed out loud. "In fact, Jim, you've been a whole lot more helpful than you can imagine."

"Sir?" But Longarm did not explain further, and after a moment the boy turned and trotted off toward the kitchen and whatever it was that needed doing there.

Longarm sat on the lobby sofa and continued to chuckle and snort long after the boy was out of sight.

153

Chapter 34

Longarm took a sip of the rye—it was good but not from the tiptop-quality bottle the bartender had poured from before—and waved to the cowboys at the corner table who were motioning for him to join them. He paid for his drink and started through the crowd toward Billy Madlock, Carl Benson, and the others.

"Marshal?" He felt a light touch at his elbow, and looked down into the bright, inquisitive eyes of the girl called Dawn.

"What can I do for you?"

"Could I talk to you for a few minutes, please? In private?"

"Sure thing. Just a second." Longarm got Jason Tyler's attention and held up a finger to say he would be just one minute, then pointed upstairs. Jason, and soon after him all the other cowboys, grinned and nodded. Hell, yes, they understood if a man wanted to take a trip up those stairs before settling down to a game. Of course they did.

Dawn led the way, and Longarm followed docilely along behind her. He suspected most of the men in the place would be watching his progress and assuming he was going with the girl to get laid. But what the hell. He didn't have to answer to anyone here, and it wouldn't matter if that really was what was on his mind.

Dawn took him into her room and closed the door behind them, sliding the bolt to lock the rest of the world outside. "Over here," she said.

Again Longarm followed. But this time he was becoming just the least bit suspicious. If Dawn wanted to talk, why was she taking him to the bed? She . . .

She wrapped her arms tight around his neck and pressed her lips to his. Her breath was warm and quick, and he could feel her tongue probing his mouth. It was not an unpleasant sensation. Not at all.

"Look, Dawn, if you . . ."

"Shh! Please. I . . . need you."

"I don't understand. What would you . . ." Again she hushed him, her mouth hot and eager on his.

"Please." Her hands were busy undoing the buttons of his shirt. And then of his fly. She reached inside his trousers and had no difficulty finding his cock. He was already hard as a tent pole in natural response to the pretty girl's attentions.

"You're so big," she whispered. "And handsome and clean too."

"Look, I think . . ."

"Shh! Please. Please." She spread his shirt open and pressed her palms warm and soft on his chest. She dipped her head and gently, slowly began to lick Longarm's nipples.

The sensations of it tingled all the way down into his crotch, drawing his balls tight and driving him half mad with pleasure as Dawn alternately suckled and licked at masculine nipples turned suddenly hard and as erect as a pecker.

155

"Does that feel good?" she asked, a coquettish smile curling and twisting at the corners of her mouth.

"You know damn good and well that it does."

Dawn giggled. And licked him again and again.

"Why?" Longarm asked.

She ignored him.

Still busy sucking and licking his chest, she began at the same time to disrobe him, pulling articles of clothing away and tossing them aside. His coat and vest and shirt first.

She fumbled with the buckle of his gunbelt. Longarm handled that for her, and draped the big Colt over the bedpost at the head of the narrow bed where Dawn worked.

"Oh, my," she whispered when she pushed his trousers down and knelt to pull them off him. "It's so pretty. So nice." She affirmed that opinion by running the tip of her tongue lightly along the underside of his cock. The thing jerked and bounced in response, and Dawn laughed happily at the reaction she caused there. "So clean. It smells nice. You know?"

Longarm suspected he did not appreciate the significance of that half as much as the girl did.

Dawn peeled his clothes off for him right down past his socks, then shed the abbreviated dress she'd been wearing downstairs.

She really was a pretty girl, he thought. Her hair was pinned back in a tidy bun and she still wore her spectacles. Nothing else now, just the glasses. They made her look bookish and prim.

Prim? Naked and yet prim? Dawn managed to make those two seeming opposites compatible.

"Fuck me now?" she said. "Please?"

She lay on the bed and held her arms up to him.

Longarm knelt between her thighs and looked down at the girl who was smiling up at him.

"Please?" she asked.

His erection was so powerful he was throbbing and bouncing, and it was no great chore for him to comply with the girl's repeated requests. He leaned forward, and Dawn reached down to capture his cock in both hands and guide it into her moist and ready depths.

Hot flesh enveloped and delighted him, and he held himself still once he was socketed deep inside Dawn's slim body.

He held himself motionless, poised there while her vaginal walls pulsed and clenched to give a sense of movement where there was none.

She lay as still as he was, and yet the feeling between them was as if her hips were pumping and her body writhing.

"Good?" she asked.

"Better than good," he acknowledged. "You already know that."

"I like to hear it anyway."

"All right. You are good. Very good."

"Do I please you?"

"You please me very much."

Dawn smiled. And began to rotate her hips in a slow, circular pattern that had his cock doing a most delightful dance within her.

"Shall I . . . ?"

"No," she said. "Hold still and let me do this."

Longarm nodded. And did as the girl asked.

Her movements were subtle. Soft. Marvelously calculated to please.

Much of the feeling came from the unseen but maddeningly powerful contractions inside her. She had a degree of muscle control that went beyond reason. But then logic and reason were not what this was about.

"You like it?" she asked again.

"It's wonderful."

The compliment seemed to be what she wanted most. She smiled and sighed. And moved beneath him.

"Hold still," she warned. "I can feel you moving."

"I can't hold still no more, dammit."

Dawn tried to frown at that, but he could see the pride and the power in her eyes. She was proud of her ability to take him past his ability to control himself. It seemed to be what she wanted. "Hold still," she ordered. But he could see that she knew he could not and that she was glad that he could not.

"Now!" he cried out, lunging forward. Impaling her on the hard spear of his pleasure. Driving bone-deep inside her body.

He bucked and shuddered and was sure he could feel a quick, convulsive response in Dawn's flesh as his own climax spilled beyond containment and his seed spurted hot and milky into her womb.

The girl cried out at the same time he came, and her nails dug hard into Longarm's shoulders.

She wrapped her legs around his waist and rode him like a bronc-buster breaking a strong colt to saddle.

Longarm stiffened, his wild plunging halted along with the flow of his juices, and after several tremulous moments collapsed on top of her.

He felt drained, utterly spent and exhausted. "That," he said slowly, "was damn fine."

Dawn sighed, her expression languid and dreamy, and pressed her face against his neck. Her breath was warm and soft there.

"Thank you," she said.

He thought about asking her. First the other day. And now this time. She was a whore. She screwed God

158

knows how many men every day of her life. And yet she was the one who wanted, insisted, that he take her.

And not for money. She had not been paid either time he was with her.

There had to be a reason why, of course. He could not begin to understand what that reason might be. A resemblance to a loved one in her past? A fantasy figure that took her into a better world of make-believe? He did not know except to know there had to be a reason, whatever that reason might prove to be.

But to ask her outright? He decided not to. Talking about it would only confuse him. And possibly cause pain to Dawn. She might not even consciously know herself what it was that impelled her to seek pleasure in this stranger's arms.

Whatever it was, she was a joy to be with. And that, after all, was all he really had to know about it. He had pleased her quite as much as she pleased him. That was enough.

He kissed the girl's forehead, her eyes, finally the softness of her mouth. "Thank you," he whispered, and for whatever reason he could see small tears well up jewel-like in her eyes.

He hated to leave her now, but he would have to go soon. He had work to do downstairs. Serious work. A few minutes more and then he would go. But not quite yet. For this quiet, gentle moment he would continue to hold and to stroke and to reassure her that she was not alone, that he was with her and appreciated her and was pleased with the great gift she had given to him.

"Thank you," he whispered again, and received in return a hug and the spill of her tears.

Chapter 35

"And the dealer takes three," Longarm said, tossing his discards aside and sliding three cards off the top of the deck that rested on the table in front of him. "What's your bet, opener?" he asked without looking at his draw.

"Check," Ronnie Gordon responded.

"I bet a dime," Carl Benson put in.

"See your ten and up five cents."

"Call," Longarm said.

"I'm out," Billy Madlock decided after a pause for deliberation.

"Call," Ronnie said.

"Call."

"Is everyone in?" Benson laid down a full house, eliciting a round of groans.

"This is your night, Carl," Longarm told him.

"About time too. Speaking of time, I suppose you'll have to hurry to catch your man now."

"Why is that?" Longarm asked.

"You know. The tracks will be open again soon. Whoever murdered that whore can get away."

"No, he can't," Longarm said as he pitched a nickel into the center of the table to ante.

160

"No? But I thought . . . I mean, you haven't arrested anyone. Have you?" Madlock's young face twisted with consternation. "Surely someone would have said something about big news like that even if you wanted it kept quiet for some reason."

"Nope," Longarm agreed. "No arrest yet." He cut the deck for Billy's deal, and leaned back in his chair while he took a cheroot from his pocket and began to trim the twist with exquisite care. "Tomorrow morning," he said as he struck a match and applied the flame to the blunt end of the cheroot.

"What about tomorrow morning?"

"Tomorrow morning I'll nail down the fellows who killed that girl."

"There's more than one?" Ronnie asked.

"I'm sure of it," Longarm told him.

"And you'll catch them tomorrow morning?"

"That's right." Longarm gathered in his cards and tipped them up so he could see. Two pair, kings and sevens. It could have been worse.

"I'll open," Jason Tyler said. "Five cents to get this game rolling."

"Who is it, Marshal?" Benson asked. "C'mon, you can tell us."

"Who killed her? Oh, I don't know that yet. Won't until tomorrow morning, like I said."

"I'm confused. If you don't know now, what makes you think you'll find out come morning?" Benson persisted.

Longarm smiled and gave the boys a wink. "Can you fellows keep a secret?"

"Of course." The four pals leaned expectantly forward, all ears now, their poker hands forgotten in the excitement of the moment. The marshal was about to let them in on a secret of his trade.

"Now that the storm has eased off, I can apply a new technique the Secret Service has come up with."

"What d'you mean, Marshal?"

"You've heard of the Secret Service, I suppose? Properly speaking, they fall under the Treasury Department, while my boss and me work for the Justice Department. Same government, though, so they shared this technique with the rest of us. They worked it out as a tool they can use if somebody ever again tries to assassinate a President of the United States. That's what the Secret Service does, you see. They protect the President. Other stuff too, I suppose. As for my crowd, it's their newly developed technique that interests us."

"Technique? What kind of technique would that be."

"I can't explain exactly how it works. We aren't allowed to do that. But the upshot of the deal is that they've worked out this technique . . . it's real scientific . . . that identifies each individual human being. You can use anything of his. Or hers. Works just as good on women as it does on men. They tell me it's foolproof. And it works on any part of the person too. Hair, spit, fingernail cuttings, anything at all."

"You're kidding."

"No, I most certainly am not. You examine any tiny particle of . . . well, of any damn thing. You have to examine it close, see, under a microscope. And the instrument has to be absolutely stable. It can't wobble or vibrate even the least little bit or this technique won't work. That's why I couldn't do it so long as the wind was blowing like it did. Even a house with a perfect foundation might wobble enough to throw everything off. But now that the wind is quiet, I can bring out my instruments and take readings off all the samples I can find out at that cabin where the girl was killed. It don't matter what I examine. If the guys left a speck of pecker cheese behind, a pubic hair, if one of them took a piss or spit on the floor, just anything at all . . . I got 'em cold. I can not only identify them, I can get the evidence to stand up in a court of law. Think of it, will you. One unnoticed hair picked up off the blanket that girl was wrapped in and some dumb son of a bitch will go to the gallows.''

"The gallows, Marshal? For killing a whore? Come on now. We all know better than that. It isn't like it was a regular person that died. The girl wasn't but a lousy little whore.''

"We all know better, do we?'' Longarm scowled. "It might've worked like that. If the killers hadn't been so god-awful stupid. I mean, right in the beginning, just after the girl died, whoever done it could have gone to Mayor Parminter and confessed. Claimed she died by accident. You know there wouldn't have been any fuss, likely not even any formal charges. He'd of had an inquest, if that, and let it drop. But whoever did it, they walked away and tried to hide what they done, and that made things serious. Then they compounded their stupidity by trying to kill me. You may not realize it, but that's a federal offense. The government takes a kinda dim view of anybody that tries to kill a federal officer. And then, if all that wasn't bad enough, the dumb sons of bitches went and burned down that livery stable. Endangered the whole town when they did that, and broke a good half-dozen state and local laws in the process. No, boys, whoever is on the string for this thing is more than likely gonna hang for all the trouble they've caused. And I will get them started on their way to the gallows myself, personally, come daybreak tomorrow morning when I collect my samples from that cabin.''

"Why don't you go get them tonight?'' Billy Madlock asked. "Wouldn't that be the sensible thing to do?''

"It might, except I wouldn't be able to see everything as good by lamplight as I can in natural daylight tomorrow. Besides, the microscope requires an awful lot of light to work right, and I have to be able to testify in court that I conducted the examination right by the book and that every tiny detail was followed. There can't be any mistakes allowed when it's a man's neck on the line. I owe that much consideration to whoever the dumb bastards are that are gonna swing for these crimes."

"Damn, Marshal, that's really interesting."

"Yes, but mind, you promised me to keep this just amongst ourselves. Don't go whispering it around, not even to your very best friends."

"No problem about that with us, Marshal. We all *are* our very best friends, all of us right here together."

"All right then. Uh, where were we in the card game?" Longarm puffed on his cheroot and leaned forward, trying to concentrate on his play.

Inside, though, he was about to get a bellyache from having to hide his laughter.

Good Lord, these dumb kids were buying it. He couldn't believe it. Gullible? He reckoned. Surely anyone with half a grain of sense could recognize that there wasn't, there couldn't be, any such "scientific technique" as what Deputy Marshal Custis Long was describing. Individual identification. What a dumb fucking idea. Hell, anybody knew that blood was blood and spit was spit and peter fuzz was just all peter fuzz.

But these boys were buying the yarn lock, stock, and barrel, and Longarm thought that was one of the funniest damn things he'd come across yet.

He'd made the whole thing up himself, starting with the germ of an idea planted by way of Jim Jennison Junior's innocent comment about criminals leaving an identifying mark behind.

And before midnight, Longarm figured to spin his windy tale not just for these happy-go-lucky—and hopefully loose-lipped—cowboys but for every bartender, rummy, or talkative salesman whose ear Longarm could find and bend.

Yes, sir, before long he expected most of the population of Kittstown to know that a brand-new advance in science would be applied come daybreak and that tomorrow there would be arrests made for the murder of the pretty little whore named Nancy.

Chapter 36

Shit, he wanted a smoke. Bad. It was bad enough being cramped and cold and miserable. But the worst thing was not being able to smoke. Dammit.

He'd been huddled inside a nest of blankets borrowed from the Jennison Arms for—what? Three hours maybe? Two at the very least. And it was getting to him that he couldn't risk the smell of the smoke or the bright pinpoint of light that the coal would give off. Not if he wanted his prey to come to the bait.

Longarm was situated well inside the wispy, ghost-like screen of winter-naked crack-willows that grew near Darby Travis's cabin.

From this hiding spot he could see both the front and the rear of the place. And one of those, he figured, should pay dividends before the dawn.

His reasoning when he made up that wild tale about a newly developed scientific technique was that he probably could rely on Nancy's killers to run true to form.

And what little he knew about them so far included, along with a willingness to commit murder, a penchant toward arson as a means of resolving their difficulties.

So what better method of destroying the "evidence" Longarm claimed would be collected at daybreak than to burn down the cabin where that evidence was to be gathered.

Longarm figured he had way the hell better than even odds that sometime before first light his killers would mosey by and torch the Travis place.

Or try to.

Longarm might have something to say about their likelihood of success.

But then they wouldn't know that.

In the meantime, though, well, it was pretty damned uncomfortable sitting motionless through the night, surrounded by snow and with air temperatures somewhere south of zero.

Worth it, however, if Nancy's killers dropped by as planned.

Longarm stifled a yawn, and made some faces to try to keep himself awake. It would have been a hell of a lot more convenient, he bitched and groaned to himself, if the sons of bitches had been considerate enough to put in an early appearance.

Longarm sat bolt upright, jarred wide awake by the presence of a new sound. Then, grumpy and frowning, he slumped back low to the ground once again. He could hear footsteps approaching, all right, but not from town. Something was wandering slowly along to his right, toward the empty plains north of Kittstown.

The sounds of snow crust crunching underfoot were clear as bells ringing in the snow-muffled silence of the night. Step-step, pause, step, pause, step-step. It was most likely a deer browsing the willow shoots for bark, he suspected. Not likely an elk, not down this low and this far from the safety of the high country. And not

167

likely a strayed horse or cow either. Either one of those would be smart enough to stay close to home and a feed trough in weather like this.

Longarm shifted in search of a more comfortable seat—but not a warmer one; he'd long since forgotten what warmth felt like—and worked up some spit to swallow in the hope he could ease his scratchy throat and avoid coughing. A cough would be as bad as a cigar to warn off the killers—or spook passing deer—and alert the whole damn neighborhood to the fact that things in this vicinity were not as lonesome as they seemed.

He ducked his head and rubbed the tip of a nose that had lost feeling more than an hour ago. Before long, dammit, he would have to start worrying about the first blush of dawn creeping up behind his back.

If this made-up ploy of his didn't work, what the hell was he going to do next to try to work out who it was that murdered the girl?

The sad truth was that he didn't have the least idea what to try if this failed.

Damn it!

He scratched his nose again, tried to rub some feeling back into his ears . . . and stared open-mouthed and incredulous when he realized that it wasn't some wandering buck he'd been listening to for the past couple minutes.

Under the black velvet canopy of the night sky, lighted almost to brightness by the wide and gleaming swath of the Milky Way and with the three jewels in Orion's belt sinking low to the horizon, he could see dark shadows moving over the stark white of the snow to his right.

And it wasn't any deer he was looking at.

There were two distinct forms. Man-shapes both of

them. Skulking along slow and coming from the exact opposite direction from what Longarm would have expected.

If he had set himself to guard the front of the place he never would have been able to see them.

As it was, however, they were clearly outlined in silhouette against the pale background.

Two men, he saw.

One of them, the one in the lead, carried a stubby weapon that had every appearance of being a short, double-barreled shotgun. Now where had he encountered anything like that before, eh?

And the other man, following close behind and moving in virtual synchrony with the other, as precisely as infantry marching at drill, was burdened with something that surely did look like a two-gallon coal-oil can.

Well, my, oh, my, Longarm thought with considerable satisfaction. What do we have here? And just what might these gents be doing tonight? Out for a moonlight stroll? Just happened to pass near to the Travis cabin? Sheer coincidence, their lawyers would claim. Hell, yes.

Longarm's lips thinned in a grimace that held no mirth whatsoever.

He sat silent and still. Content to bide his time and let these jehus demonstrate their intentions beyond the possibility of reasonable doubt.

Chapter 37

The two dark figures, each bundled heavily in coats and gloves and mufflers, made their cautious approach to the back of the cabin. The one with the shotgun, slightly the shorter of the two, stood facing outward to keep watch, while the other one went about the business of dowsing the logs of the wall with coal oil, starting about waist high and letting the volatile fluid pour over the logs thoroughly.

Actually Longarm was not sure that would be enough to destroy the place even if he left them alone with their task. The thing was, Darby Travis, or whoever it was that built this cabin, had used thick, unsplit, but completely peeled logs for his construction.

With no bark to act as tinder, and as difficult as it is to set a thick chunk of wood aflame, there was some doubt—in Longarm's mind anyway—as to whether these fellows were very adept when it came to arson. Like as not, he figured, the coal oil would burn itself out harmlessly on the surface without getting the logs started.

Not that he was going to offer any helpful suggestions

for improvement, of course. All Longarm needed for his purposes was to see a match flame. From there on, any court in the country would be forced to conclude that conflagration was what these gents had in mind.

And sure enough, there was the fire as the one with the scattergun said something to his partner, and the taller one struck a match.

Longarm was thirty, forty feet away, and could hear the sounds of the whispered conversation without being able to make out the words.

He thought the voice was familiar, but could not have sworn to that.

And anyway, he had everything he needed now.

Staying low behind the screen of willow withes, he first took aim with his .44 and then announced, "Don't neither one of you move. You're both under arrest. You with the gun, drop it. You with the match, hold still."

Dammit, that was what a peace officer was supposed to say. Billy Vail drilled that into all his deputies often enough.

But just as pretty nearly always happened, the book that said an officer was supposed to announce himself didn't get around to guaranteeing that the asshole idiots would go along with the instructions.

Hell, they almost never did.

And these fellows were no exception.

The one holding the match dropped it. The one with the gun held onto it.

The taller one quite naturally tossed his match onto the coal oil he'd just finished pouring, and a gout of bright flame leaped up the wall, illuminating the men and everything for a dozen yards around them.

The shorter one brought his shotgun to bear, searching in the sudden flash of light for the source of Longarm's voice.

171

Longarm didn't know for sure if the guy with the gun could see him or not, but he was not much inclined to take chances with a man who'd tried several times already to shoot him.

Longarm's Colt barked, and a slug took the one with the shotgun high in the middle of his chest. Just about at the point where his heart ought to be.

The man teetered backward, righted himself, and went down face-first in the snow, the shotgun discharging harmlessly into the ground as a convulsive grasp of dying fingers closed on the triggers.

"You! Hold still, dammit."

"Yes, sir."

"Hands up."

"Yes, sir."

"Now kick some snow onto that fire and knock it down."

"Yes, sir." The man held onto his oil can with one hand and bent to sweep some snow onto the fire.

At least that was what Longarm thought he was doing.

Instead the fool grabbed for the shotgun his partner had dropped.

"Dammit!" Longarm snapped.

He thought the dead man had already tripped both triggers of the scattergun. He thought the thing was empty and harmless. He thought.

The problem was that he did not know that for certain sure.

And he wasn't willing to bet his life on it.

The man picked up the shotgun.

Longarm put a bullet into his forehead.

The man dropped like a marionette with its wires cut.

"Shit," Longarm growled, stumbling forward on legs numbed by the combination of freezing cold and long inactivity so he could dowse the coal-oil fire and remove the threat to Darby Travis's home.

Only when he was done with that did he take time to see just who it was he'd shot and killed this frosty morning.

"Aw, God *damn* it!" he complained once he saw.

Chapter 38

Back-trailing the two dead men to where they'd started from was about as difficult as following a pair of street-car tracks down the middle of Colfax Avenue.

Longarm didn't know what the hell they'd intended to do about the deep set of footprints they'd left behind with every step they took. Pray for more wind and snow? Could be. The truth, of course, was that they really hadn't had much choice about it.

Not if they'd believed Longarm's lies about that new scientific technique that would finger them as murderers. Believing that, they'd had to go through with trying to destroy the evidence and save their necks, and never mind small details like leaving footprints behind.

As it was, of course, the trail in the snow was so plain Longarm didn't even have to wait for daylight to follow it. He simply ambled along in their path, not even having to break trail for himself. They had already gone and done it for him.

The path led a half mile or so to a small dugout gouged into the side of a low hill. The dugout looked old. It might have been someone's line camp at one time, or even the site of a failed homestead.

Whatever it used to be, now it had been fixed up with some fresh sod on the roof and a windbreak of piled stones in front of the leather-hung door.

A plume of smoke lifted into the sky from a sheet-metal chimney at the back of the low roof. A lean-to had been built to serve as a storage shed. Longarm took a look inside—surprises were not something he craved at the moment—and found it filled with saddles, bridles, and similar gear waiting for springtime.

Longarm sighed. There wasn't any point in screwing around here. Better to get it over with.

And there wasn't any need to be subtle either. The men waiting inside would be expecting someone.

It was just that it was not Longarm whose entrance they anticipated.

He made sure there wasn't anyone outside in the crapper. Again, no surprises were wanted. It wouldn't much do for someone to come up behind him with a gun in hand, say, or even a billet of stove wood that could be used for altering the shape and the contents of a man's skull. Then he simply walked over to the door and let himself in, Colt already in hand.

"How'd things . . . *Jesus!* You."

"Uh, huh. Me."

"But where . . . ?"

"Madlock and Benson are both dead. I was waiting for them at the Travis place. They were stupid. They tried to shoot it out with me. I suggest neither of you boys makes that same mistake. I do this for a living, remember. You'd be in way the hell over your heads."

Jason Tyler was lying on a bunk with a pile of blankets tucked chin high. Ronnie Gordon had been feeding wood into the stove when Longarm interrupted the chore.

"Did you . . . I mean, how'd you know it was us?"

"You want the truth, Tyler? I didn't. Oh, you boys were on my list of possibilities. Naturally, you all being young and horny and broke until you could start drawing pay again. But I tell you true, son. I didn't think it would be you four. I thought better of you than that."

"But how . . . ?"

"Why was I laying in wait this morning? Son, I told that story all over Kittstown so anyone interested in keeping track of the rumors would know I was gonna make my arrest today. And whoever was guilty . . . I didn't have to know who that was . . . whichever sons o' bitches was guilty would just naturally figure they had to come out and destroy the evidence before I could get to it."

"You trapped us."

"I did that for a fact, yes."

"That isn't fair, you know."

"Neither is murder. Nor the assorted other things you've done."

Ronnie Gordon stood and shook his head sadly. "I can't . . . I can't face going to the gallows, Marshal. That would purely kill my folks. They're decent people. They wouldn't understand."

"Rape. Murder. No, those things are kinda hard for decent folks to accept. Maybe you should of thought of that before you killed that girl."

"I didn't . . . me and Jason didn't have nothing to do with that, Marshal. It was all Billy and Carl. They're the ones raped her. It was Billy Madlock that beat her to death. I'll swear to that, Marshal."

"So will I," Tyler put in.

"Reckon you can tell that to the judge. Mayhap he'll even believe you."

"You don't, Marshal?"

"I told you, son. I do this for a living. Do you think

176

I've ever once arrested a guilty man? Of course not. They're every one of them innocent. Pure as the driven snow, like the saying goes. Just ask 'em. They'll tell you.''

"Marshal, I mean it. I can't hang. I just can't.''

"That ain't up to me, Gordon. A judge and jury will take care of that.''

"I just can't. I really ca—''

Gordon whirled and grabbed for a battered old Sharps carbine that was leaning against the wall beside him.

It was a crazy thing to do.

But then the choice was clearly his. And he did indeed mean that he couldn't stand to swing. He would rather accept the alternative than the disgrace.

Longarm obliged the young fool with a bullet that hit him high in the throat and sprayed the hot stove with fresh blood. The blood sizzled and stank, filling the dugout with a sickening stench.

Longarm scarcely noticed. Jason Tyler was still alive. And Tyler's hands were underneath his blankets where Longarm could not see what they might be busy doing.

The muzzle of the big Colt was aimed unwavering on a spot just about a half inch above the bridge of Tyler's nose.

"God, don't shoot me, please don't shoot me, Marshal, please.''

"Stick your hands out from under those covers,'' Longarm ordered.

Tyler's hands appeared with a magician's speed. They were empty. And shaking.

"Now kick the covers back.''

"Anything you say, Marshal, just please God don't shoot, don't shoot.''

The smells of saltpeter and sulfur from the burnt gunpowder fought to overcome the equally strong stink of the scorched blood.

Longarm felt a mite queasy himself under those combined influences. And they were too much for Jason Tyler. The terrified cowboy puked all over the front of his long underwear. But he didn't take his hands down even then.

"Why'd you kill her?" It was probably a stupid question. Shit-for-brains criminals virtually never told the truth. Not about hardly anything, including their own right names. But it was a question Longarm had to ask anyway.

"She . . . it was an accident, like."

"An accident?" Longarm moved close behind Tyler, clamped one steel cuff onto Tyler's left wrist, and jerked the arm down so it was held at the small of the cowboy's back.

"We were on our way to town. For a drink, play a little poker, you know."

"Uh, huh." Longarm brought Tyler's right hand down as well and snapped the other cuff in place, securing his hands behind him.

"We saw her coming toward us. Just walking slow and looking all around. Kind of . . . enjoying things. You know?"

"Yeah. I know."

"We'd about used up our pay already . . . a run of bad luck . . . but the last we went over to Norma's place Billy'd had this Nancy, and he liked her real well. He said we all ought to have a go at her, so we stopped her and asked. She got all snotty with us. She said no, it was Sunday and she wasn't working. If we wanted to fuck we could come to the whorehouse later on sometime and she'd give us whatever we wanted. Well, what we wanted was to have some pussy right then. And we didn't like some little bitch whore like that saying no when Billy'd already fucked her once and she said herself she'd take us on another time. I mean, that made us mad. And Carl, he grabbed her first. I think it was him anyway. It was kind of like once we got started, we all got into the spirit of it.''

"Uh, huh," Longarm said again, restraining an impulse to kick Tyler in the back of the head. It was easy to kill someone that way. Real easy.

"And we were right there close to Old Man Travis's place and we knew he wasn't home and . . . well, we dragged her in there. So nobody could hear her shouting, see. She was screaming her stupid head off. And it's not like she was some damn virgin faced with a fate worse than death. She was a whore, for God's sake. A lousy stinking whore. Where did she come off telling us we couldn't have any.

"So anyhow, one thing led to another. We all of us screwed her. A couple times each, I guess. But she wouldn't shut up. So Billy hit her, to get her to quiet down, like, so we could leave. But she wouldn't leave it be. She was hollering crazy stuff, like how she was going to have the law on us for rape. Well, that was a laugh. We all knew better than that. But then she did a really dumb thing. She kicked Billy. Square in the balls. God, that pissed him off something awful. I mean, it would have made me that mad too. So he punched her. Just as hard as he could. And then he hit her again, and Carl hit her and Ronnie and . . . and I kicked and hit her some too. I mean, we all did. We just . . . forgot, kind of, what we were doing. And the next thing you know, she was dead. We hadn't meant for her to be. Honest. It just . . . happened.''

"Yeah, sure."

"We laid her out on the bunk, and Ronnie was the

179

one that closed her eyes and folded her hands and tried to make her, like, presentable. Then Carl took her handbag. She had some money. We spent that, of course.''

"What did you do with the bag?'' Longarm asked.

"We burned it. We didn't want . . . you know.''

"Sure. Evidence.''

"That's right. We didn't want any evidence around. I think Ronnie kept the little coin purse she had with her. We shared the money, but he liked the coin purse. Said it would make a nice tobacco pouch. So he kept it. It's, um, in the saddlebags under that bunk in the corner there.''

Longarm took a look. The coin purse was there, all right. Just as Tyler said, whatever money it had contained was gone by now. What the purse still held were a St. Christopher's medal and a scrap of paper folded into a small wad and tied with a bit of string. Longarm untied the paper and spread it open: "IN CASE OF ACCIDENT PLEASE NOTIFY . . .''

"Come along, you piece of shit,'' Longarm instructed.

"What about . . . you know?''

"Your buddies? Shit, I dunno. Maybe somebody will come along and bury them. Or maybe the buzzards and the raccoons will get to them first. I don't much care either way.''

Jason Tyler shivered. And he did not so much as ask for a coat or blanket to cover himself before he hurried out into the cold dawn of his first day of incarceration, the first day of the rest of his life.

Chapter 39

"Afternoon, marshal."

"Good afternoon, Mr. Bonner."

The Union Pacific conductor touched the brim of his cap deferentially. "Off to Denver, is it, sir?"

"Not this time, Mr. Bonner. I'll be staying with you all the way to Omaha."

"Is that so, sir. Well, we will have to see what we can do to give you a nice trip the rest of the way."

"Thank you, Mr. Bonner, but it isn't a pleasure trip."

"No?"

"No, I'm . . . you might say that I'm taking a friend home."

"I see, sir."

Longarm rather doubted that the gentleman did see. But there was no point in explaining.

The thing was, Nancy *would* be going home.

Nancy Anastasia Gruenwald. Loving daughter of Hans and Hilde Gruenwald of Fremont, Nebraska. He'd already wired them. They would be waiting in Omaha. Waiting to take Nancy back into the arms of her family.

The pity—one of many, actually—was that they were doing it now.

The pity was that they hadn't done it when it might have meant something.

The pity was that Nancy herself would never know.

Or would she?

Longarm frowned and swung up the steel steps into the coal-heated warmth of the U.P. passenger carriage.

He selected a seat and reached for a cheroot, forgetting for the moment that none had yet been shipped in over the newly opened tracks and that he would not be able to buy any more until they reached Laramie, maybe even Cheyenne.

He did not look back to Kittstown.

There was, after all, nothing back there that he cared to remember.

Watch for

LONGARM AND THE INDIAN WAR

220th novel in the exciting LONGARM series
from Jove

Coming in April!